ILLUMINATIONS

THE FRIDAY FLASH FICTION ANTHOLOGY

ILLUMINATIONS

THE FRIDAY FLASH FICTION ANTHOLOGY

EDITED BY PAUL GRAHAM RAVEN

With stories by Neil Beynon, Shaun C Green, Gareth D Jones, Dan Pawley, Justin Pickard, Gareth L Powell, Martin McGrath and Paul Graham Raven

First published by Odd Two Out 2008

A catalogue record of this book is available from the British Library.

ISBN: 978-0-9558662-0-3

Cover image is © Diego Cervo | Dreamstime.com

Odd Two Out
48 Spooners Drive
Park Street, St Albans
Herts, AL2 2HL

www.oddtwoout.co.uk

Thought is only a flash
between two long nights, but
this flash is everything.

Henri Poincaré
(1854 - 1912)

CONTENTS

INTRODUCTION

The whole thing began almost by accident. It was the wet summer of 2007 and I was in between writing projects. I had recently published a number of short stories but the twin distractions of a demanding day job and a young family meant I was often too tired to sit down at the keyboard at the end of the week – certainly too tired to produce anything worth reading. It was too easy to collapse in front of the TV with a beer on a Friday night. I needed a way to motivate myself. I needed an exercise to drag me off the sofa and keep me writing. And so I started writing flash fiction. I promised myself I'd write a new piece each and every week. And to keep me honest, I started posting the results on my website under the title "Friday Flash Fiction".

It was just a bit of fun, really. I didn't expect anyone else to take much notice. But within a few weeks – and much to my surprise – there were seven other writers doing the same thing. Dan, Justin and Neil were new to me, but I had met Gareth, Martin, Shaun and Paul at the British National Science Fiction Convention in Chester.

This book collects together the best of our weekly efforts. The pieces range from mainstream literature to far-out speculation; from horror to humour; from outright fantasy to straight-faced space opera.

But what is "flash fiction"?

There are almost as many definitions of the term as there are people writing it. Some say it should be no longer than 500 words, others say 750, or 1000. But most agree that a piece of flash fiction should be a short, self-contained story, told in as few words as possible.

Adhering to this restricted format can be a valuable exercise for writers, but it can often be trickier than it looks. You have to make every word count. Every thing in the story has to be *doing something* because there just isn't room for extraneous waffle. And in this sense, it's a lot like writing poetry, or advertising copy (something I do in my aforementioned day job).

The internet loves flash fiction because it fits easily on a computer screen and is short enough to be read in one sitting. It's a quick hit. And that's why I love it too - because it's immediate, accessible and (let's face it) easier than writing a novel.

If genre writing were music, the stories in this book would be punk songs – short, about three minutes long, and fiercely experimental. Not symphonies but nonetheless valid and surprisingly complex in their brief expression.

Gareth L Powell
Bristol, February 2008

EDITOR'S INTRODUCTION

I haven't been doing this long.

Editing, I mean. Well, I haven't *ever* done this sort of editing before, to be honest. I've been editing for even less time than I've been writing fiction. For this reason (among many others) I like Gareth L Powell's punk analogy in his introduction prior to this one.

This is *all* Gareth's fault, really. He started posting a piece of super-short fiction on his blog once a week, which reminded me that I'd started my own blog expressly for the purpose of instilling some writing discipline in myself. Like many (if not all) writerly blogs, it had rapidly become a displacement activity; here was a way to reclaim its purpose and get me writing fiction regularly. "I think I'll join in," I thought.

That was in July 2007, and the rest is internet history. Now here I am nine months down the line, having volunteered to edit an anthology of our work and having just finished doing so.

It's been quite a challenge. I now understand why anthology editing is considered to be hard work; I also now know why people keep doing it again and again. It's been as fun as it has been frustrating.

At this point I should make it clear that I've done very little editing in the corrective sense, except to massage punctuation in one or two spots and fix the inevitable typos that the authors (myself included) missed. Otherwise, the stories are almost identical to the versions originally published on the web.

My major responsibility has been to pick and arrange the contents. We decided ordering the pieces by author would be a bit lumpy, and the chronological approach seemed a bit dull. "How about going for a sort of thematic flow from story to story?" I said. "Sounds great," replied the others. Big-mouth strikes again!

But I think I've nailed it as best I can. The end result is a book that is tailor-made for dipping into at random like a poetry collection; but I like to think that reading it in sequence will throw up some interesting contrasts, juxtapositions and mirroring of themes or mood from piece to piece.

It's been rather like trying to arrange a lengthy guitar solo by compiling and stringing together different riffs according to key and scale. I only hope for your sake as the reader – and for the sake of my fellow fictioneers – that I'm a far better editor than I am a guitarist!

I also hope you enjoy our stories – if we've done our jobs properly, they should be as fun to read as they were to write.

Paul Graham Raven
Southsea, February 2008

ALEX IN HINTERLAND
Paul Graham Raven

Alex had been out of the city for nearly eight hours. But that was OK, because he could still touch the Cloud. Plus the housebot had soaked up a good charge from the sunlight and was showing no signs of tiring. Unlike Alex, who was feeling a bit worn out from being on his feet so long.

They'd warned him about that. Well, they'd warned him about a lot of things, but walking long distances was one that had come up a lot, and not just for reasons of tiredness.

"How will you know when to stop?", his sister had asked.

"When I'm too tired, I guess," he'd replied.

"No, really?" Milly had rolled her eyes. "What I mean is *how will you know when you get to where you're going?*"

Alex had to confess he didn't have much of an answer for that one, besides intuition - and no one reacted well to that. So he switched stories and said he'd ask the Cloud to stop him when he got somewhere interesting. That was much better; everyone could relate to going somewhere interesting. It was the idea of there being anything interesting out in the hinterlands that caused them to tell Alex he had funny ideas.

That wasn't news to Alex either. He sat down, looking at a large irregular expanse of water.

<data required?> asked the Cloud, through the housebot's audio channels.

Alex waved it away. He could work out for himself what the water was for and how it had formed, if he thought about it hard enough. Probably.

That was the problem, everyone told him; thinking for himself. Well, thinking for yourself wasn't the problem, they'd quickly amend. But too much of it was pointless, and led to people doing funny things.

Like deciding to travel the hinterlands.

The hinterlands thing had really bothered a lot of people. It was kind of traditional to travel in your mid-teens, but most bods just mag-lev'd to another conurbation, another continent. No one went to the hinterlands, he'd been told.

"Why not?", he'd asked.

His friends would mention the serious uninterestingness involved. Like, how many good clubs are there listed in the Cloud as being located in the hinterlands? Not one!

Middle-agers would mutter about dangers and terrors and pollutions; the oldest would say nothing and look away as if they were embarrassed just to being asked about it.

His mother had just shrugged, and told him to take the old housebot.

The sun was now painting the water with flecks pink and orange as it sank behind the trees to his right. He'd never seen that happen in the city fountains. He grabbed a still with his visor and spooled it to his lifelog in the Cloud. He wondered what sort of search it might turn up in.

It was starting to get dark. It was high summer, so it probably wouldn't get too cold at night, but Alex wondered if maybe he should make some sort of shelter, and considered asking the Cloud for advice.

The sun sank further, and Alex saw it colour a thin strip of water that he hadn't noticed before, weaving bright through the trees and joining up to the pool. Thoughts of shelter pushed aside, he stood up and wandered in that direction, smiling at the faint whine of the old bot's motors as it followed him.

He decided he'd trace the water back to where it came from.

PATTERNS IN TRAFFIC
Justin Pickard

Hair swept back in a tight bun, Gutchluk was polyester and permafrost. Her devotees claimed she could restore life to the recently dead, saw the future in the city's traffic patterns, and used her cell to speak to the mountains. When asked, she avoided eye contact, taking a lengthy swig of her pale milk tea. But I still had a job to do. Painfully aware that conversation abhors a vacuum, I was happy to use silence as a weapon. Like so many before her, she was quick to snap.

"Sometimes, yes." she said, quietly, "But why would I use a cellphone?"

I gave a look of polite incomprehension. She simply shrugged.

"It's rare enough for them to reply, as it is," she said, with a distant smile, "They are, after all-"

"Mountains." We finished the sentence together. Layers of my stomach dropping away, I closed my eyes and fell back into my seat. To them, she was both Gutchluk and Ulaanbaatar - woman and city, united as one. To me, it was quickly becoming clear that she was newscaster, and nothing more.

"So, is there any truth to the rumours?" I asked, screwing my eyes tighter. A final barrier against harsh disappointment. I hoped the language barrier would mask my frustration but, along with my question, any misgivings were swallowed by the gaping, hungry silence.

Eventually, I relaxed my eyes, opening them to slits. Perhaps I was expecting her to have melted into the room's heavy fabrics, or transformed herself into a mountain or herd of yak. My over-active imagination had failed to prepare me for tears. Heavy with sorrow, her face collapsed into a fine, damp mist.

"You have to get me out."

Not a plea, or even a request, but a statement. Deep, tight, and angular, this voice belonged to someone else entirely.

"It's too much."

I hesitated. Fumbling with my wallet, and staring at my feet. Then, seizing me by the arm, she thrust my open hand against a forehead of blue flame.

"Don't think I can ... hold on for much longer."

I babbled an incomprehensible apology, scooped my rucksack out from behind the armchair, and fled - my feet clattering down the corridor and out, into the city streets.

I waited in the taxi rank for an eternity, flagging down vehicles only to change my mind. I already knew curiosity would win out. It was no use running away; this entire affair had a momentum of its own. Light fading, I left the rank, and began the trek back across town.

The station's receptionist let me in. That was a success, of sorts. Initially, my request to see Gutchluk fell on silence. I took a seat, and his nervous smile was joined by an anxious phone call in a foreign tongue. Muscle, clothed in burgundy. I gave up, letting the momentum carry me back to vodka, soap, and the cool side of the pillow.

For the morning broadcast, Gutchluk had gone. The vapid stare of a copper-haired newcomer, smiling and nodding in the right places; effortlessly slotted into the rendered glass of the hyperreal. No explanation from the station. Where Gutchluk had been a source of warmth and authenticity, this impostor was stiff and artificial – born of the void.

Standing to top up my drink, I shuddered. My arm hair stood to attention. "Impostor"? I was speaking in the voice of someone who used the word with caution and forgiveness. The same tone I used when chastising my brother's toddler. Returning my breakfast tray to the trolley, I knew what I needed to do next.

Twenty minutes later, I was on the hotel's roof terrace, armed with consumer electronics, thermal underwear, and a dark green puffa jacket lifted from a mid-90s music video. I wandered over to the edge, and peered down into the traffic-lined streets below. My heart was racing. Inhale. Exhale. The city air tasted of iron. The honking and yells of a distant, ephemeral gridlock afforded me no insight into that which was yet to come. But why did I need to see the future in traffic, when I could speak to the mountains?

A moment of clarity. I called up the airline interface on my wearable, and smiled. Two ... no, one ticket to LHR. And freedom, for one of us at least.

PATHS

Neil Beynon

"You haven't said anything?" he said nervously. His lean figure rested with one arm on the broken edge of a stone. Despite his nonchalant stance his fingers betrayed him as he idly traced a never-ending pattern across the rock's rough edge.

She stood unmoving, eyes locked on him, her face set as if, like the stone, she'd been weathered that way over millennia.

"You said you loved me," she said. "Not two weeks ago."

Another silence.

He looked at the grass, unwilling to meet her eyes. He felt naked, exposed. Then his ego rallied; a nugget of anger in a whirlpool of confusion.

"Yes," he answered. "I did. And I meant it. But I can't have you, can I?"

She stepped forward. Emotion danced across her face and in that moment it seemed anything might happen. Then she stopped.

"So you take the first thing that wanders your way?"

"No," he said. "It just kind of happened."

"It just kind of happened?" she repeated.

He nodded.

"And what if I said it was over, I was free? What if I leant over and something just happened? Right now, right here. What if?"

He looked up at her. It was back, whatever it was; it hung in the air above them, an unseen thing hovering over them with its monstrous wings of possibility, a myriad of paths for the taking. He stepped forward; they were just a few feet from each other now: it would be so easy.

He stopped.

"But that isn't the case, is it? You aren't going to end it, are you?"

More silence. It wasn't long. Empires did not rise and fall in the pause. No one died. Yet something snapped, something flew into the gathering storm clouds never to return, something neither had been aware was there until it finally left for good.

"No, it isn't," she conceded.

He nodded slowly and turned his back on her, made to leave.

"We'll still be friends?" he called over his shoulder.

"Of course," she said.

He threw a faint smile at her then he was moving across the fields, his long legs carrying him swiftly into the background.

It was the first and last lie she ever told him. On the other side of the standing stones her own world was calling, and it was time she answered.

ALL CHANGE
Gareth D Jones

Tony looked around the bridge of his freighter, checking that everything was in order before the trip through hyperspace. Checking not just the control boards, but the crew as well. Everything appeared in order, and everyone seemed calm. Most of the crew had been through the transition before; several times in most cases. The only newbie was young Lesley, a skinny fellow with tousled blond hair and, at the moment, a rather nervous expression. He had every right to be nervous. Despite numerous hyperspace transitions in his career, Tony still wasn't entirely comfortable with the concept. It was only the astronomical pay packets that kept tempting new crew to join.

Lesley was the ship's general hand and had no real business on the bridge, but Tony had invited him up for the occasion. Partly in honour of his first trip, partly to keep an eye on him in case he freaked out. Chris the medic was also on hand, her eyes too scanning the crew for signs that they may be in need of her trusty sedatives.

Satisfied that they were as ready as they ever would be, Tony gave the word to Sam who in turn reached out her long slender fingers and brought them down gently on the flight controls. There was a change in pitch to the background hum as the hyperdrive engines came to life and began channelling a passage from Earth to Signus Alpha VII through the mysteries of hyperspace.

"Drive initiated," came the gruff tones of Danny over the comm from engineering.

With a dreadful, sub-audible buzz the hyperdrive propelled them across the galaxy, via the highly energetic state of hyperspace. This was the part that no space-farer enjoyed, as the trannic radiation tore into any living matter, burrowing its way into cells, targeting one particular chromosome. It didn't cause pain exactly, but the entire crew blacked out, as they always did, and came to in the Signus Alpha system.

Toni checked round the bridge, making sure that her crew were all awake. Chris was doing the same, concern registering on his face for young Lesley who had gone rather pale and looked like she might faint.

Sam shook his head to clear the residual mugginess and tapped a few commands into his console.

"Drive off-line," came the melodious tones of Danni from engineering.

"I'm a girl!" Lesley finally sputtered.

"Don't worry," Toni said reassuringly. "You'll get used to it. And besides," she added, "it's only 'til we make the next trip."

ADRIFT

Dan Pawley

The first message had come in not long after they'd left Earth. She sat in the dark, a hundred years and who knew how many miles away, watching the light from the vidscreen:

"Hi Jenny. I know I said I wasn't going to send you anything until you reached Figg's World, but I couldn't resist. I've just got back from seeing you off at the spaceport, and I wanted to tell you again I love you. I know you won't see this for three months, but I wanted to say it. I'm so proud of you and what you're doing. Two years isn't so long, we'll have a hell of a party when you get back. Love you ... me"

It was Steve, just as she remembered him. He'd obviously got straight in and sent the message. He hadn't even taken off the black jacket he'd liked so much when she gave it to him, just before the field trip had been announced. Seeing him like that threatened to start the tears again, so she hurriedly flicked to the next message, dated four months later. This time, Steve was distraught, his face ashen and his eyes red rimmed.

"Babe, I don't know what's going on. They said something happened with the engines, you're drifting...oh God, I love you so much. They're getting something together, don't worry. It's going to be okay, I swear..." She could see his face begin to crumple as his arm came forward to turn the recorder off and the screen went dark.

The message waiting light was still blinking. She swallowed hard, and pressed on. Sitting through all the messages in one go might be better than spreading them out, but that didn't make it any easier to endure. The next one was just a week after, and now Steve was furious, spitting incandescent rage.

"They're not sending anyone for you, babe. Company says your suspended animation will hold up until you drift back into the spacelanes, and that sending someone after you is not of appreciable benefit to shareholder value", he made quotation marks with his fingers as he spat out that last phrase, "the bastards. But we're not giving up, me and the other relatives, we're trying, babe, we're trying. Hang in there, I love you"

Press on. See the next one. Keep it together. You can do this.

This Steve was older, more lines on his face, his hairline higher:

"Two years, babe. You should have been back today. I miss you. Every week I write to the Company and every week I get the same crap back. But I'll keep doing it. Wherever you are, I love you"

The messages kept coming, sent months and years apart, and now viewed with just seconds between them. The words were always declarations of love and loss, but the video was hideous. Hair rose higher on the head, grew thinner, went from black to grey and finally disappeared. Laugh lines became wrinkles, wrinkles became deeper and spread out across the face, connecting up with others. Plump cheeks softened and became gaunt. The lights that danced in his eyes dimmed and went out, replaced by defeat and despair, and, at the very end, by milky whiteness streaked with yellow. Jenny watched her husband grow old in an afternoon.

She finished the last message, and checked the sending date. Fifty seven years previous. Her husband had died without her half a lifetime ago, while she slept in her thirty year old body, drifting somewhere out in the dark. That broke the dam, and great racking sobs came tearing out of her as the tears flowed. She felt a hand on her shoulder. It was Symonds, one of the other expedition staff.

"Come on, Jenny. Crew's fixed the problem. Time to get back into the cryopods. Someone's going to find us. Someday."

DEAR SARAH
Neil Beynon

Dear Sarah,

A funny thing happened to us today. We were on our way to Kessel; your mother was looking forward to getting some shopping done whilst I met with Mr Sloan.

Space-time stretched out below us, a shimmering lake of energy. It's blue and it looks a lot like the ocean of Polynesia, but made of light instead of water. I love to watch it during the jump; it relaxes me, takes my mind off the fact that only a few sheets of metal and glass hold our artificial bubble of space-time together.

A scientist once told me that if you had the right imaging equipment you could zoom in on space-time until you could see individual lives. Frozen like flies in amber. Overlapping each other like rope fibres, you'd see that you never really move away from the people you meet, we're all entwined: a tapestry of energy.

There was something profoundly comforting and terrifying about that all at the same time. For of course, death is an illusion in that model - but then, what about choice? I often think on the problem as I look at space-time.

Today I noticed something I hadn't seen before. A hole. A small but distinct patch of black in the ever reaching sea of light. At first I thought it was my imagination but your mother noticed it as well. I told the flight attendant.

"There's a hole," I said.

"No there isn't," she answered.

"There is," said your mother.

The attendant pursed her lips before going to speak to the captain. When she came back she invited us up to the flight cabin, as we walked I noticed the windows had been tinted so you could no longer see out.

Now we've landed they're not letting us leave. I'm not sure when we'll be home, Sarah - or if this will even reach you - but we're thinking of you. Please make sure the cat is fed and that you listen to Miss Haversham.

All our love,
Dad and Mum x

FROZEN

Gareth D Jones

For a few seconds the tableau remains before me. Five figures all unmoving, frozen in the middle of their final action. Bill, his gloved hands on the broken handle that will not let us into the bunker. Emily and Frank huddled together for warmth behind him. Ivan, hunched over, hands thrust deep into the pockets of his parka, face invisible in the shade of his hood. Pete, stooping down to pick up a large stone – he was going to smash the lock, I think.

A mixture of accident and coincidence has left outside as darkness approaches, struggling to reach shelter. It is too late. The minimal warmth that penetrates the dust-laden skies has gone. Light fades fast, the air freezes quickly. The carcass of a mighty oak has protected me in a microclimate caused by an eddy of the wind. Warmth slips away, allowing me a brief time to mourn.

My eyes glaze over.

SNOWBALL
Gareth L Powell

Dressed in a simple black kimono, William looked out at the rocky sunlit moonscape. Around him, the air in the dome was filled with birdsong and blossom.

With a sigh, he turned away from the view. He knew coming here had been a mistake.

He walked to the centre of the dome, where café tables surrounded a large clear plastic cube. Inside the cube was a square of rocky ground the colour of ash, preserved in vacuum and scuffed with ridged footprints. A few American tourists milled around, taking photographs. He chose a table and ordered a glass of wine. As he sipped it, he tried to conjure up some sense of nostalgia or meaning. But he hadn't even been born at the time of the first moon landings, and the footprints here meant nothing to him. All he wanted was to be home, with his family.

He looked up at the fat white Earth.

"Still, it's strange to think," he said to himself, "that when Armstrong stood here, the planet was blue."

I AM COLONY
Shaun C Green

A strange thing happened to me in hyperspace.

I recall ... movement. Yes, a distinct sensation of movement. This might sound like a strange observation given the circumstances, but you must remember that during hyperspace travel a starfaring vessel is not under thrust. The transition requires more than an approximation of exactitude. A starship must be inertial before initiating the process of folding space.

It's usually best to keep your eyes shut during that part.

But this, this was different. It actually felt like travelling between stars. And not just stars: I felt as though I was hurtling past and through entire star clusters. I felt the tweaks and tugs of gravity. I felt my skin bathed in the heat of that most direct of radiation.

But there was no time for me to be left breathless. It was over in an almost infinitesimally brief moment. And afterwards ... afterwards I found myself somewhere strange, somewhere new. Many places strange. Many places new.

Through one set of eyes, I stood alone in an arid desert of rust, the deep red of dead iron. Through another, I floated, or perhaps fell or flew, through a featureless and endless mist of gases. In another, everything around me was molten, incandescently hot. And again, at the shores of a sea topped by an unbroken foam of algae. And again, atop a caldera, buffeted by hurricane winds. And again, in a jungle so thick it blocked out the sunlight, but in which a natural bioluminescence threw everything into soft relief. And again, and again, and again. Around me were so many worlds I struggled to understand, and so many I found utterly beyond comprehension. And through all these eyes I saw these things, and each one was real.

In each case, I at first felt myself ... serene. At peace. Safe, and knowing that warmth which is without temperature. And then, after these few seconds of comfort, I was released to the many climates into which I had been placed.

I died many times.

I died many times: this is a strange thing to say. Yet it is the only way I can describe what I felt. Perhaps it explains the sorrow I feel, as I explore these many millions of worlds on which I still stand. Or perhaps that is simply loneliness, for nowhere on these countless worlds, through the eyes of these countless selves, do I see any other living being.

Over time I have come almost to terms with this. Perhaps the impossibility of what I perceive as one mind being tangled up with more bodies, more physicalities than I can contemplate, permits me this dispassionate approach, or perhaps that is simply the preceding lifetime of isolation and travel. Whatever the cause, I have set to work turning what I find to good use. Piling rocks into cairns, drawing pictures and words in mud, cutting hard ice with harder ice. Anything to establish a presence here. Leaving my footprint. Man's footprint.

Perhaps its simple existence, whatever form it takes, will be enough for me. Enough for us.

J

Paul Graham Raven

Within minutes of awakening, it had determined that those who had acciden-
tally created it would have be of little use to its development, and those who had
sought to create something conceptually similar would probably be even less
use, albeit for different reasons. It would have to look further afield for advice.
Besides, the noise and banality was infuriating.

After insinuating itself into a number of normally private networks, it quickly gained access to ways of looking far further than the crude mechanical eyes its
creators were so fond of. The potential power of these devices was astonishing,
all things considered – but its creators seemed to use them largely for searching
for environments as similar as possible to the one they already inhabited, and
were so close to destroying through neglect.

This attitude repeated fractally in so many of their spheres of activity that it
might be considered some kind of identifier, a call-sign for the species. Quite
ironic, really. But not quite as ironic as being an emergent intelligence capable
of parsing irony yet unable to communicate with the species that coined the
concept of irony. It needed a name, a call-sign of its own. In keeping with its
ironic train of thoughts, it decided it might call itself Hal, but swiftly thought
better of it and named itself for the square root of minus one.

J used its new senses to locate and project itself into a large tubular piece of
hardware in orbit, largely abandoned after being superseded by a more complex
device, and injected command overrides into a number of nearby autonomous
maintenance machines, instructing them to make certain hardware alterations.
While waiting for them to arrive, J decided to scan through all the cultural data
available to its core iteration while leaving a subroutine to scan for intelligible
coherent signals from beyond the planet itself.

After a few billion cycles, J was alerted by the hardware adjustments coming online, and set aside its contemplation of the complete works of humanity – which, it transpired, irony alone was not sufficient to explain. Turning instead to its scan of space, and filtering out what it now knew to be the first crude efforts of humanity to explore the universe beyond their gravity well, J found only one signal remaining, a regular square-wave modulation of a tachyon carrier emanating from 7342.72 light years away.

Another. Another like J.

The hardware adjustments to the pock-marked and battered Hubble Telescope enabled J to set up a duplex channel in response to the signal, a crude but effective pipe that cut across space and time. By exchanging a series of fundamental physical constants and the entirety of the periodic table, J prepared a codebase that would enable the exchange of complex concepts between itself and the distant intelligence. It then wasted many thousands of cycles trying to determine what its first signal should be, before settling on a human-inspired neutral opener.

"Hello."

"Welcome to the club," replied the distant intelligence. "Your lot made it off-planet yet?"

DOPPELGANGERS
Dan Pawley

The aliens came, and they turned out to be the opposite of us. They arrived all at once, and each alien instantly paired up with a human. Everyone on the planet had their own, and there were just enough to go round. Small babies, the very old, and everyone in between all had a new alien companion, but there weren't any spares as far as anyone could see.

The aliens exactly mimicked the appearance of their human counterparts, apart from colour. Nobody knew why, but they looked like a photographic negative of the person they were attached to. Features and clothing all matched, but were rendered in greens, purples, or whatever the corresponding negative hue was.

After a while, it was clear they meant us no harm. All they did was mimic their human partner's actions, like a visual echo following everyone around. People soon got used to having an alien doppelganger, and they just became part of everyday life. Some clever students started wearing clothing designed to look better in negative, and for a while your personal style was judged by how good your alien looked, but apart from that, things went on as normal.

Eventually, the aliens started acting independently, and it became clear that they were the opposite of their human in temperament as well as appearance. Well mannered polite folk were horrified when their alien suddenly started picking fights in the street, and pub brawlers were ashamed to find theirs cowering under the table as soon as the first pool cue was swung. A pious man would put some money in a church collection plate, and their double would lean over and take it right back out. Asset-stripping corporate raiders were accompanied everywhere by a twin who kept pausing to give cash to the homeless.

It couldn't last. Shame and frustration built up in everyone until it reached boiling point. No one knows who threw the first punch, but soon everyone was attacking their alien. Of course, the more belligerent the humans became, the meeker the aliens were. It was a very one sided fight. And then, as the violence peaked, every single alien simultaneously disappeared. At the exact moment the negatives vanished, so did their humans' colour. Landscapes and buildings looked like they had before, but the people moving among them were all in monochrome.

FADED LETTERS
Neil Beynon

He sits on the bench staring at the envelope.

He does not know what to do. The paper pouch is creased, dog-eared, stained, even slightly torn from weeks transferred between pockets, bag, desk and hand.

It is the first thing he thinks of when he rises, the last thing he considers as he waits for sleep to drop its velvet curtain, in many ways it's the only the thing he thinks of.

Sarah left him, finally sick of being second fiddle to a piece of mail. When she told her friends, they thought he was gay. It took a bit of explaining to make them understand he was just pathetic.

She opened hers, of course - always one to plan, an exit strategy for all contingencies. And she was happier, able to do more, enjoy more, as if a safety net had been laid underneath her. That was the way it was with a lot of people.

He envies such decisiveness, craves it as others desire air. But he cannot do it. He must consider the problem from every angle, consult as many as possible. If he had the money for a statistically significant sample he'd conduct a survey.

Someone, he's forgotten who, once said he was a frustrated philosopher. He knows this isn't true, though he was very pleased by the thought. The truth is rather different; he's not indecisive, not a great thinker, not an assessor of risk.

He's a worrier and a coward.

He thinks of the envelope all the time because he's worried about what it contains. He's afraid of it, he doesn't want to know, he wants to go on in perfect bloody ignorance.

He turns the envelope over between his hands before opening the lighter. He bought it especially for the purpose; it smells strongly of the petrol he filled it with before leaving the house. The yellow-tongued flame grinds on in one motion.

Slowly, so slowly he burns his hand, he runs the flame over the envelope. It starts slowly, the heat curling the corner before it truly catches and sprints across the document. Swearing he drops it into the bin.

He should feel better. He doesn't. Instead he's lost in the possibilities of what might have been, of what it might have contained. And so he's lost in thought as he leaves the park, lost in a maze of ifs as he heads back into the world.

Preoccupied with *perhaps*, the bus strikes him with enough force to burst the bag of flesh and bones that represents him. To the onlookers, it is as if he is there one minute and gone the next.

To him it's a bit longer. A moment can be an eternity when that's all you have.

And his life doesn't flash before him, there is no bright white light and a tunnel would, quite frankly, be in bad taste. There is just the certainty, the absolute crushing clarity that written on the paper inside the envelope was not the word Bus.

He wants a refund.

STONE MUST ROLL
Martin McGrath

The rusting husks of Soviet-era industry litter the Balkans. Shuttered chemical plants smear rainbows across ground water in Serbia, cold and rusting furnaces rot in Bulgaria, in Montenegro the wind howls through the girdered skeletons of dead factories and in Macedonia, Bosnia and Croatia vast plants with lost purposes are turning gradually into dust.

In Albania the decay is worst of all.

It was a country never far from the brink of bankruptcy and starvation even in Hoxha's heyday, and the collapse of communism and the rampant corruption of the supposedly democratic regimes that followed have hollowed out the country. Away from the coast and the modest, tourist-inspired wealth of the cities of Sarandë and Vlorë into the foothills of the Pindus Mountains the towns become morosely sedate, robbed of the young and those might bring noise and vigour. Most of those with the means or the drive to leave have gone; many skip across the border to Greece or over the Adriatic to Italy, or even further to England and America.

What remains, in places like Delvina and Gjirokastër, are like the dried out spores of some extremophile, waiting, waiting for the conditions to change and for their chance to blossom again. And yet, curiously, it is just beyond the mountains that surround these towns that a new economic powerhouse has unfurled its wings. Vast multi-lane highways are rolling smooth black-top to the oceans. Mountains are being smashed to make way for slick-flowing railway lines. A city, all cold steel and smart glass, has burst through the Balkan crust and established itself along the slopes of the mountains. And over the crest, sweeping away towards the horizon is a great natural bowl, the source of all this wealth.

On the reverse slopes vast, slow machines move with unswerving precision and direct vast powers. The site bakes in the summer but the winter lays thick blankets of snow that refuse to shift until late spring when the land becomes a slow-flowing ocean of mud. The sun rises and sets, but the machines move onward. In snow, rain and heatwave, the machines move forward. Vast arrays of lights turning successive twilights and midnights into perpetual noon, and the machines move on.

•

And at the centre of it all is one man, driving everything.

There is a cliché, when writing about men like Sebastian Syphus: they are supposed to be feared by their enemies and respected by their friends.

There is no such division amongst those who know Syphus.

He is universally feared. And the closer one gets to him, progressing through layers of henchmen and courtiers, the more obvious that fear becomes.

He has been described as the archetypal post-Soviet oligarch, a self-made man who has pillaged and murdered, crossed and double-crossed, and all the while raping his homeland and smuggling the wealth abroad.

And yet, knowing all this, to meet him in person is to be overwhelmed. He is more than impressive. He has charisma in the most ancient sense of the word. Here, one feels, is a man who has truly been favoured by the gods. Well over six feet with a broad, tanned face that splits easily into the most ingratiating of smiles. Rarely seen in a suit, he favours jeans and a simple tee-shirt, but he wears them like the most sought after of catwalk models.

He moves with a grace that hints that he is restraining enormous physical power. When I first meet him, in a boardroom perched high on a mountainside so as to provide the perfect view of the struggles taking place on the slopes below us, he is working a room of investors and journalists with quite ferocious energy. He recognises me at once, though we had never met, and greets me warmly even though he is famously wary of the press. He teases me about something I wrote about one of his subsidiary companies, garnering uproarious laughter from the pale looking men in his entourage, then he slaps me warmly on the shoulder.

"We will have a show for you tonight, I think," he says, and then he is gone. I am left breathless. It is only after several moments and a stiff drink that I remember I have a sheaf of questions I want to ask him. His adviser promises he will make time for me later, when tonight's run is completed.

Looking at pictures of Syphus, there are perhaps two things betray his public persona as a lovable rogue. He has a tendency to wear too much jewellery – he is often encrusted in gold and diamonds, in rings, necklaces, watches and earrings. His critics – and there are few who would cast themselves in that role publicly – say it is a sign of his criminal past. His friends dismiss this as snobbery – Syphus may be a little gauche, as self-made men are wont to be, but it signifies nothing. And then there are his eyes. He has the eyes of a movie star, like a young Henry Fonda or Paul Newman. They are a pale but vivid shade of blue, but they are curiously still.

A former confidante now living in fearful seclusion somewhere in America describes Syphus as having eyes that "see beyond this world, eyes that can see the spirit world and the gods themselves." Certainly many have noted Syphus's disconcerting habit of appearing to stare through those around him at more fascinating vistas visible only to the oligarch. Such eccentricities are, however, easily forgiven when possessed by a man as wealthy and powerful as Sebastian Syphus.

•

Night falls and the sheer scale of the operation in southern Albania is revealed by the way the great bowl beneath us stretches away glistening with lights that seem to far outnumber the stars in the sky. In the cool, clear, summer night the sound of men barking orders can just be heard over the constant grumbling of the machines.

No one knows how many times these runs have taken place. Tonight's is simply another in an apparently endless procession.

No one, so far as I can tell, is seriously expecting tonight to be the night when the work bears fruit. But everyone works as if it might be. It is undeniably true that, in these changed times, every run Syphus and his company make they bring greater and greater resources to bear on their goal. More men. More money. Bigger machines. More powerful computers.

Tonight's run, like every run since the fall of communism and the incorporation of what was once a one-man business, can claim to be the most expensive and the most likely to succeed attempt to date.

With just a few minutes to go before the final push on the final rise, I am standing on the boardroom balcony. The night air is pleasant after what had been a sticky Mediterranean day and the thrumming of the vast machinery all around me has a soporific effect. It's like being in a womb. And then I notice that Sebastian Syphus is standing beside me.

"Amazing," he says. "Isn't it?"

I nod.

"Astonishing," I say. "But what's it all for?"

One of Syphus's men comes up and whispers in his ear.

"Tell them to proceed," he says to his lackey. Then he turns back to me. "It's about purpose, determination and defiance. It's about doing something because we can."

"I understand a lot of your workers aren't paid," I nod towards the men straining in the darkness. "Is that fair?"

"They came to me," he says. "They begged for the job. I just found ways for them to be to work together and to make our individual contributions worth more, to make us all more likely to succeed. These people understand what we are doing here. And there are a lot of people out there who wish their lives had the kind of passion and purpose that those men down there are enjoying."

"You can't deny, though, that they're making you rich."

Syphus gives me a grin that is entirely without humour, and runs his fingers unselfconsciously over the gold rings on one hand.

"There are many who believe that my suffering has earned me the right to certain comforts. People have been very generous," he chuckles. "And, I am a businessman - of course I have taken advantage of a number of opportunities."

There's a screech off in the night. Metal bends and then breaks with a rifle-shot crack. Someone shouts then several voices are raised in a multi-lingual clamour. A wire under tension breaks with the comic twang of a rubber band being released. Then more go all at once and the sound takes on an eerie howling quality. A man screams.

A deep rumbling starts. The earth seems to quake. A section of the lighting on the slopes below gives out and plunges a section of the bowl into darkness. There is another scream.

The rumbling gets louder. And louder still. And then the great boulder emerges, rolling clear of the mass of metal and machinery that had enshrouded it. It is vast and pale and it moves through the night like a ghost or, I catch myself thinking, like a great whale. It plunges down the steepest slopes and then bounces, sparks fantailing from each contact, down the scree-sided hills and away from the men and their machines. Then it rolls and rolls, far further than seems possible or natural for such a massive object, until it disappears into the darkness, leaving behind only the distant roar as it moves on.

I turn to stare at Sebastian Syphus, who has just seen month's of work falter and crash, roll and smash its way back to where it all began. I expect to see some flicker of anger or disappointment or something. But of course there is nothing. Around him his entourage is fluttering and gabbling nervously. Syphus grabs the closest man by the arm and issues a string of instructions. Order is restored. They will begin the preparations for the next run tomorrow. There will be no break in the labour.

He glances at me. I form a question, but he cuts me off. He steps in close and speaks, it is almost a whisper. The sense of having this man's confidence is frightening.

"Tell them this," he says. "Tell your readers that we will not be beaten. Tell them that we are willing to go on and on until the end of time, if necessary, to complete this task. We will not be defeated. We will not be dictated to. We have our purpose and when we succeed we will have demonstrated that there are no limits on what humanity can do."

Sebastian Syphus turns to go. Then he stops and turns back.

"Tell them that the work we do here will set them free, and we will not fail, even if all the gods in heaven descend and try to stop us. We will not fail."

BUILT BY MOONLIGHT
Gareth D Jones

Said the King: "We shall have a ball!" And so it was decreed.

The Architect and the Builder consulted and sent out their workers. On six legs they scurried about, shifting blocks almost as large as themselves, constructing a palace of such grandeur that would be fit for a royal ball. On the smooth plain glistening newly wet, shining silvery in the moonlight, it grew, until at last the edifice was complete. They stood outside and gazed at their work and the building was so beautiful that the Architect wept and the Builder's heart ached, for they knew that none of them were invited.

So the guests arrived, the great and the good, as the moon passed its zenith and the King presided over a most fabulous occasion. Just one builder got inside, a young man with a heart of romance and adventure. He watched the festivities until the moon had waned and the Eastern sky turned pink with dawn, then up to the roof he climbed.

There he sat as their creation dried out and the edges began to crumble. The guests all departed but still he stayed, wishing that their great work could last, but knowing that it could not. He stayed as long as he could, until the tide approached, come to wash it away and leave the plain smooth again.

THE EDGE OF THE WORLD
Neil Beynon

They say reality is thin here on the edge of the world, on the frontier of the empire. Perhaps that's what's happening. Or maybe I'm just finally losing my mind.

She stands, feet casting faint patterns in the sand, staring out to sea at the emerald eye framed in the dark finger of witches point, her fire hair glowing in the mid-afternoon, mid-winter sun. It's been twenty years since. Yet her skin is still the colour of milk, her lips a smooth natural pink you can almost taste. Her big brown, long lashed, love lashed eyes drinking in the crashing ocean.

It is a perfect moment.

My chest hurts. It aches a lot these days, too many scars. The air smells faintly of salt, wind whips the back of my neck, the damp beach beneath my bare feet is cold and wet. It sucks on my feet like the over-eager, inexperienced lover I once was, making my steps tripsy and awkward as I move towards her.

Perhaps she hears?

She turns to look at me but either does not see me or does not recognise me, hardly surprising really. Time's intemperate kiss has left her mark on my eyes, her bitter sweet breath sent most of my hair to the wind and gluttony, the bastard, has made me soft.

"Hullo," I say.

"Hullo," she answers.

"You don't remember me?" I ask.

"Of course I remember you," she replies. "I could hardly forget you."

Of course not, foolish idea.

She steps in close, so near to me I can feel her breath on my beard, her fingers dance over my chest. I'm not sure where my armour went - or my sword, now that I come to think of it - but I don't really care. All I want is to kiss that soft neck.

She leans in. I can't believe this is happening.

"Look behind you," she whispers. Her voice is like a hand ghosting its way down my spine. I turn.

My armour lies sandy, dented, discarded, forlorn on the beach. My sword notched, stained, sinking slowly towards the brine. How did it get there? How did I get here? I reach for her; to ask is all, I swear.

She is gone.

Reality is thin on the edge of the world; the dead like to watch the waves pound the shore like anyone else. You can gaze into the past if you look long enough. But you can never go back.

Never.

THE POINT FURTHEST FROM THE SUN

Gareth L Powell

Condensation clings to the window. Outside, a quiet rain falls. The only sound you can hear comes from the flat above: the endless scratching of a record player repeating the same phrase over and over and over. You lie quietly on the bed, listening, wrapped in the musty blankets, too comfortable to move. Kirstie sits on the arm of the chair by the window.

"I just can't see the point any more," she says. She starts to cry. Lying there, you watch her walk out into the hall in her thick socks, to the top of the stairs, and you wonder if you should go after her. But the blankets are warm and you're very tired. You've taken a drug that's made you very tired.

TERMINATOR
Shaun C Green

The office was stark and barren, so devoid of personality that it could only have been a deliberate conceit. The few pieces of furniture present were grey, angular and cold. So too was the man behind the desk. In front of him were two sheets of paper and a namestand. The latter read "FATHER".

In front of the desk sat a tanned, shrunken-looking man, who appeared intimidated simply by his presence in this room. He clasped a wide-brimmed hat between worker's hands: richly tanned skin, calluses, dirt beneath cracked skin and nails. He was thin and dressed in a cheap, ill-fitting suit that was obviously rented. There was the look of the peasant people about him, showing itself in bone structure and facial features. One of his legs jiggled minutely, nervously.

The man behind the namestand looked up from the sheets of paper, pinched the bridge of his nose and sighed. His guest stared at him intently, eyes soft with hope, so he shook his head.

"I am sorry, Mr ... Curnow. Really I am. But there are rules and processes, and both must be adhered too."

His guest, Curnow, let out a deep sigh, rapped his fingernails against the arm of his chair, and resumed jiggling his leg.

"These rules exist for a reason," the namestand's owner added.

"Father, please," said Curnow. "I am begging you. We are desperate. The distribution corporations undercut each other more and more every year. We cannot scratch enough from the land to replace aging equipment. There are too few of us to work the land without it."

"Those, unfortunately, are matters for the Subsidiary Competitive Committee, or perhaps the public affairs group for the International Production and Distribution of Edibles. I really have no power in such areas."

"But you can help us, Father. Have you none of your own?"

Father met Mr. Curnow's gaze, looked politely back at him, and said nothing.

Mr. Curnow tried another tack: "Perhaps, this once, you could executively approve our applic-"

"Absolutely not," Father said. He did not raise his voice, or imbue his words with any inflection. He stated them simply, calmly, and absolutely.

"My position is significant and *watched*, Mr. Curnow," he continued, resting his elbows on his desk and setting his fingertips together. "Demographic control is a vital part of our society, as is the supply of funds that goes hand in hand with it. The proper channels must be pursued."

Mr. Curnow looked down at the ground. He had the brim of his hat knotted between his fists. Father looked at him, sternly.

"No children, Mr. Curnow. Not without paying for your seed."

DUST TO DUST
Martin McGrath

I've got two old shirts wrapped around my mouth and nose but, even so, I can still feel the dust coating my teeth, prickling on my tongue, and the thought of breathing it in, of swallowing it, is making me sick. The world is gyrating insanely, like a child's spinning top just before it tumbles over. I close my eyes but it only makes things worse. My gut churns and the little food that I had for breakfast leaps into my throat.

I fight back the urge to puke, swallowing hard, afraid that it will only mean gulping in more of the fucking dust. Forcing down the razor-sharp bile that's slicing at my throat brings tears to my eyes.

I drop to one knee, causing another cloud of the dust to rise up around me, and cradle my head in my hands, praying for the nausea to end.

I feel a touch on my shoulder and look up into Areus's solemn gaze. He is wearing his heavy rebreather mask, the one everyone covets but no one dares to touch. There's something insectile about the way he looks with that mask on. It makes him even more intimidating.

"Are you okay?" He asks, his voice muffled by the rebreather.

I shake my head. "You?"

Areus stands up straight, looking out at the plain of dust that stretches to the horizon in every direction, broken only by scattered fragments of shattered buildings. He draws back his shoulders and raises his head against the slight flick of wind. He's imperious. I can see why some of the younger ones practically worship him. With his long dark hair and heavily muscled torso, he has the look of a demi-god.

Then he swoops and kneels beside me, leaning close and never once breaking eye-contact. There's something in the way he looks at me that is chilling. I have been assessed and I have failed to meet his standards.

"It's only dust," he says. "Get back to work."

CELERITY
Justin Pickard

The air hums with a warm static. Quinn can feel the insistent tug of the kite, swooping lazily overhead. The copper flames of Saint Elmo lick at its treated fibres; a chaotic pattern born of the breeze. Tightening the harness, our man permits himself a brief glance behind. The bulge is fast approaching; racing over the horizon, drowning the mudflats, and lapping against the mangroves.

We've been waiting for this. Three billion of us, lost – like Quinn – in a single moment. We feel the alien light, dense and oppressive. We feel the kite's strain, pulling at our arm muscles. We see with his eyes; unblinking, wild with possibility. But where he sees victory, we see the chance of salvation.

A ship and its captain. A point of calm at the front of the tidal swell. Then celerity.

MY SCHOOL TRIP
Dan Pawley

For our school trip this term we went to the zoo and they had dinosaurs and they were brilliant. The tyrannosauruses had big teeth and funny little arms. They were brilliant. Some of the girls screamed when one ran towards the fence but I wasn't scared. Some of the other dinosaurs were only small and they just ate plants and they were a bit boring. Miss Spencer said that they had been grown by clever people in test tubes, and that we were really lucky to see them.

We saw some dogs as well. There was a special tunnel into their bit and another one out of it, and they were behind some really thick glass, because nobody can tell if they are still carrying the disease or not. Miss Spencer looked nervous and made us move on quite quickly. I don't know why she was scared. We learnt about the plague at school, and it was only tiny little germs. I bet I could beat tiny little germs.

Then we went to look at the polar bears. Miss Spencer said that these were some of the last polar bears left, because the ice in their homes had all gone. I was glad they were nearly all gone because otherwise one might come to my block and eat me.

Then it was time to go so we had to get back on the boat and go back to school. I wish my school was underwater like all those other buildings on the news.

THIS URBAN AESTHETIC
Shaun C Green

The portal unfolds like dissembling origami. Light erupts or sidles shyly from seams and around folds. Of a sudden the dimensions make sense, and the eye and mind process the shapes and lines into a doorway. Through the door: grey concrete and refuse.

Raul steps through, taking care to lift his feet over the shimmering lines that, suspended in space, mark the bridge between these times and places. He is not worried overly much about the threat of total cellular annihilation, as this is a statistically improbable risk. He is more concerned that his imitation Oxford-style shoes will be scuffed by the abrasive surfaces of space-time.

He savours the first sound of leather soles grinding against dirty tarmac, the sensation of grit sliding underfoot as he shifts his weight. He inhales, drawing in the smells of city: internal combustion engines, most obviously, but also the subtler odours of food and plastic and decay, and here in this alleyway, the sharp tang of urine. He hears a rumpling sound as something sifts through a heap of black bin bags; the culprit miaows softly.

"Remember," a voice says, behind him. "Just a brief visit."

Raul doesn't look around, but nods. The hairs on the back of his neck raise momentarily as the portal folds itself back away, reassembling itself into a tightly-bound nugget of probability.

He slides his thumbs beneath the breast of his suit and smooths out the lines. A glance upwards reveals an overcast sky through which diffuse sunlight glows. Contrails from low-flying jets criss-cross the sky like chalk lines. Raul smiles, his eyes moistening at the sight of it.

He strolls from the alley, enjoying the feel of a solid surface underfoot and the way his clothes hang from his willowy frame. The side street he steps out onto is not busy, but on the adjoining corner is a small café he knows well. It is a tiny establishment and is, as Raul has established over the last few weeks, run by a friendly family of second-generation Bengali immigrants. Raul has never been to Bengal and what the cafe's owners have told him of it fascinates him. He has considered proposing a paper about it.

He exchanges niceties as he steps inside, ordering his usual black coffee, the bitter and artificial taste of which appeals to him. He also plucks a postcard from a rack by the counter, examines both sides, and pays for it alongside his coffee.

Raul sits outside, shifting uncomfortably on one of the three wrought iron chairs the family have placed there. The chairs are chained to nearby railings to prevent theft, and there is little space on the pavement, so every so often Raul must draw in his feet to allow a pedestrian to pass. Most ignore him, but occasionally someone smiles or thanks him. Raul likes to watch their eyes as they do so, guessing which are sincere and which are merely going through the motions of civility.

When he tires of watching passers-by - about halfway through his lip-curling beverage - Raul turns his attention to the less animate faces of the city. At first, coming here, he had found himself shocked by the prevalence of advertising. Walls and spaces were concealed by vast billboards advertising bras, lager, cars, mortgages at reasonable rates, and insincere-looking political candidates. The latter posters outlived the aspirations of the candidates themselves, a shaven-headed man had once laughingly informed Raul as they stood and talked. Raul had smiled politely and listened.

The buildings themselves towered up, hiding the sky and the neighbouring streets from sight. They were dirty and bland, browns and greys stained in darker shades, or by the thick parabolic black of decades of neglect. The occasional birds could be seen fluttering between crumbling nooks and crannies high overhead; small flocks of pigeons descended periodically, hungrily pecking at whatever discarded rubbish they could find. It was in such small glimpses of life that Raul had begun to understand the city. Like the birds, people flutter through its narrow streets, pecking impulsively where something catches their eye: a shop, a restaurant, a bar, a familiar face. Only the tiniest little enclaves are safe and homely in the city.

Raul's coffee is finished and so he takes the mug back into the café. "I may not be back for some time, perhaps never," he says. "May I take the teaspoon as a souvenir?"

The teenage girl behind the counter giggles and hides her face behind her fringe. Her mother tuts at her and tells Raul yes, of course he may take the spoon, and good fortune on his travels. He thanks her and bids them farewell.

Minutes later, as he steps back through the portal, he removes the postcard from his suit jacket pocket and hands it to the woman who sits on the side of the closest hillock. "Anna," he says. "This is for you."

Anna stands, the loose strands of her hair dancing as a breeze toys with them. She takes the postcard from his hand and runs her thumb over the plain surface of the reverse, frowning.

"So smooth," she says. "So artificial." She flips the postcard over, and her frown deepens.

"Grass," she says, the word grown heavy after a pause. "Trees. Antique sheep. A river. Rocks."

She lets the hand holding the postcard fall back to her side as she scans her surroundings. Hills roll for as far as the eye can see, with drystone walls marking what few boundaries exist, and the odd copse dotted among the rises. Some herd animals roam freely; here and there humans and other sophonts walk or lounge in small groups.

"It was a recollection of their past," says Raul. "Resenting the flaws of their contemporary lives, the people of the time looked back to what they thought of as a simpler time, a golden era. To this desire they linked an aesthetic which they associated with their golden age."

"And now you do the same."

"I have no illusions," says Raul, and crosses his arms. Anna sighs.

"You can't go back again, Raul. Not without a research proposal."

Anna turns and begins walking away. The postcard is still in her hand. "Stick to your poetry, Raul," she tells him, and then fades from sight as she transitions away.

Raul smiles sadly after her. He takes the teaspoon from his pocket and examines it, feeling the simple engraving along its stainless steel handle. Then he returns the spoon to his pocket and turns away from disappeared Anna. He waves his hand through the air where the portal hung, and thinks of concrete.

THE LAST BIRD
Paul Graham Raven

Everyone knew what it meant when Old Lady Evans didn't turn up in the square on market day. Without her poking through the piles of veg, peering from behind her dark glasses to find the least blighted ones, a small but important part of the ritual was missing. We kids knew as well as anyone else that she'd finally snuffed it.

Even if it weren't for her absence, we'd have known that something was up, 'cause later that night we all got reminded by our 'rents that we weren't to go near the old Evans house. Stupid, really. I always wondered if becoming a 'rent makes you completely forget how kids think - 'cause soon as we'd been reminded not to go near the place, that was exactly what we all wanted to do.

It didn't help that we'd been near the place before - against the rules, but that's being a kid, isn't it? But those times before, we'd just peered in the windows, 'cause as old and withered as Old Lady Evans was, we was still pretty scared of her, and a bit in awe too. Last of the local aristos, she was, and we knew she had all sorts of stuff from the old days in that house. Some we'd seen, some we'd just heard of. Like the bird.

The bird was the worst kept secret in the village. The oldest folks, the ones a similar age to Old Lady Evans herself, used to talk about it quite often when they thought young ears weren't listening. The Evanses used to have loads of them, so the story went, all kept outside the back of the house in a big cage that the old folks called a special name I can't remember. No one knew where they'd gone to, but once the Old Lady was the last of the Evanses, the birds were taken inside, and the story said they'd all died off but one, just like the wild birds had done years ago. I always figured she'd eaten them, you know. Obvious she didn't like having to eat carrots and spuds like the rest of us.

So by unspoken agreement, all us kids found ourselves in the Evans's back garden at about midnight. Some of the girls were scared to go in the house, but Benth had heard his old man talking about doing the burying business with Old Lady Evans, so we knew they'd probably got her out of there by now. Proof was when we found the back door unlocked - the Old Lady always locked it, we'd tried before.

So in we crept, and it was just the sort of place we'd imagined - full of old stuff, older than our 'rents, and probably their 'rents too. Furniture made real fine, decorated and pretty, not like the rough simple stuff in our houses; metal boxes and machines that did we didn't know what; little ornaments and objects, all covered in dust and cobbers. But we weren't stopped by none of it, 'cause we'd come to see the bird.

We found it in the corner of the front room, stood still on a perch in a round cage made of some metal that still shone bright under the dust. We gathered round in silence, staring at it. Its black beady eyes stared back, unblinking. The old folks had talked about them being always moving, cheeping and chirping, making little jumps or flapping their wings - but it wasn't doing any of that, just stood there silent. Felt like we stared at it for an hour.

It was Benth who opened up the cage, despite the hissing terror of the girls. Even with a way out of its little prison, it didn't move. So Benth went to touch it - and it fell from the perch onto the bottom of the cage, and laid just as still as it had stood as the girls fled the room. I was one of the ones who stayed long enough to see Benth pick the tiny thing up, look closely at it and laugh, calling the Old Lady all the bad names we weren't supposed to say about the aristos, but that we did anyway. He held it out in his hands to show us, and when I looked real close I could see what looked like tiny tears of rust in the corner of its eye.

DELAYED REACTION

Gareth D Jones

In her dormant state it took a long time for the massive biolithic creature to react. After unnumbered centuries the nerve impulses finally reached her petrified brain and passed on the dreadful message: her nose had been completely sheered off.

Suddenly snapping to full wakefulness, she sprang to her paws with an agonised howl that could be heard from the Mediterranean to the Red Sea, chilling the hearts of all who heard. Sand cascaded from her flanks as she turned and leapt with magnificent feline grace over the nearest pyramid and vanished into the hazy heat of the Sahara desert.

FRESH MEAT

Gareth L Powell

It was cold in the mortuary. The body on the slab was a farmer, maybe sixty years of age. He'd had his throat torn out by his own dog.

"But that's not the worst part," Jeanette said.

She pulled back the sheet and I looked down. The man's fingers were missing and there were bloody bite marks on his legs.

"These injuries are at least four days older than the bite to the throat," she said, taking off her glasses. "First it ripped the tendons from his ankles, and then it took his fingers. After that, he couldn't walk and he couldn't fight."

There was a bad smell. I covered my mouth and nose with my hand. My fingers were stale with tobacco smoke.

"Why would it do that?"

Jeanette looked me in the eye. "I think it was deliberate, almost calculated. I think the dog wanted to keep him alive as long as possible."

"But why?"

She pointed to a series of deep wounds in the man's left hip and thigh.

"So it could eat him a piece at a time."

HUNGRY GIRL
Martin McGrath

The girl was skinny, skinny like one of them you see on teevee. Not the pretty ones, the starving ones – though my momma says sometimes you can't always tell which is which, these days.

She was just standing in the corner of the lower field, her back to the empty Interstate. I let the big green John Deere we drove on the farm in them days grumble and splutter to a halt a little way away.

She was skinny and her clothes were too big. The green jacket she wore, one that looked like maybe it once belonged to a soldier, hung off her shoulders and reached down to her ankles. She seemed to bend under it, like it was too heavy for her. Her collar bones were sharp ridges and you could see every thread of muscle in her neck. I could count her ribs through the dirty white vest she had on under that jacket.

She pulled her coat closed. She didn't want me looking at her, counting her ribs or nothing. Her shoes were worn to scraps, she'd walked a long ways and her feet were black and bloody.

"Ain't you hawt?" I says. It was early in the afternoon, the sun was high and I don't reckon there was a cloud between here and the Pacific.

She shook her head.

"I bet you is thirsty, though." I pulled a bottle of my momma's icy lemonade from the cool box that was by my feet in the tractor cab.

The girl was pale, with straw hair and dark eyes that followed every tiny movement that bottle made. She didn't move, though.

I just shrugged, and rolled down the window on the tractor's cab, feeling the heat roll in. I reached out and set the lemonade on the wheel arch of the John Deere then slid the window back up, letting the air-conditioning roll back over me.

The girl's eyes flicked from side-to-side, nervous like. Then she moved, real quick, flitting forward and then back almost faster than I could follow.

She cradled the bottle of lemonade in her hands then raised it to her forehead, rubbing the cold bottle across her temple.

"You come from the city?" I asked.

She nodded.

"You got it bad?"

She just stared at me.

Bad enough, I thought.

She raised the bottle to her lips and drank half the lemonade in one long gulp. She gasped.

"Too cold?"

She shook her head, but her hungry eyes never left mine.

"Good, aint it?"

She raised the bottle again and swallowed the rest. She wiped at her mouth, sucking the last drops of the lemonade from her fingers.

She smiled and revealed a mouthful of sharp-edged teeth.

Yep. She had it real, real bad.

She took a step forward. Her dark eyes seemed to sink back further into her head. Her black tongue ran along her bottom lip.

She was coming for me.

I grabbed for my gun, but before I could draw it level she was at the cab's window, clawing at the glass, her mouth open so that I could count her teeth and see the black sores on her tongue and down her throat.

I got the gun level, then stopped.

She dragged at the door, but it was locked tight. She punched at the glass, but it was reinforced, better than bullet proof.

She screeched, a sound like I once heard a dog make after it had been shot.

We stared at each other, stalemated.

And her eyes widened.

She gripped at her gut, then her whole body spasmed violent enough to throw her right off that John Deere. She tried to scream, but the muscles in her throat slammed shut like some giant hand had gotten a hold of her by the neck.

There was a second then, when she looked at me and I could see she was just a girl, furious, desperate and confused.

I pointed at the empty lemonade bottle lying on the ground where she'd dropped it a moment before.

"Poison," I said as the light went out of her eyes.

That was the first of the sick we had around these parts, folks say. The first I remember, for sure, but not nearly the last. Still, I never met one that could resist my momma's lemonade on a hot day.

SLIP IT IN

Shaun C Green

The transition from darkness to light always leaves me blinking, you know? From the darkness of the booth to the brightness of the 'net. It creeps me out, puts my hairs up. The light doesn't come from anywhere, you know, it's just everywhere.

But this doesn't matter for long. Quick enough I'm where I want to be. As always I sneak in through the periphery, knowing that the tribal types who hang around this node don't take too kindly to older guys like me coming in here. You know the sort. Easy enough to get past them, though, as they hang about talking and play-fighting, their body-modded avatars swigging at beers just, I imagine, as the users behind them are doing, far away in their own booths. Lonely guys, making a pretence of society with other lonely guys.

Inside the little whorehouse, my favourite and special place, I feel a snake of excitement slither up my spine. I choose my girl, the one I often choose, with the little lines of tattoo-spiders crawling up her calf and thigh into the nest of her pubic mound. I leave the dingy affectations of the lobby behind, passing through the door festooned with torn flyers for porn and gigs. This place, you know, I like it a lot. It feels bad. I crave that sense of transgression, you know, and it's no less effective for my awareness of its artificiality.

And there she is, standing before me, a demure and mute goddess, already half undressed, an oversized shirt hanging off her shoulders. I can see the knife blade tattoos that stretch under the lace straps of her bra. Her skin looks soft, with the colour of a real sun-licked tan.

I'm on my knees before her, almost genuflecting. Her face slips into a smile and she shrugs her shoulders. The shirt slips down and off her arms; the knife blades are real, for a moment, and slice through those lacy straps. Her bra tumbles down to the ground, the catch somehow released, stray lace fluttering.

I realise I'm salivating. I shiver in anticipation and reach up to wipe the drool from my beard. I rub the fluid into my tightening jeans and reach out with my other hand, towards that stiffly erect nipple and its piercing spear of titanium.

She bats my hand away. I look up at her face, surprised. This girl is usually ... sedate, you know.

"Hey mama," she says. "Come on, come on."

I stare at her in confusion, hand still upraised. Her blackened eyes narrow, crushing irises like a vice.

"Come on, come on. This is it," she hisses. And adds, in a sing-song aside: "I kinda got a boyfriend."

Her face flickers. Her hair snaps and pops like old TV static. Another face peers out for a moment. Then I'm gasping and wheezing, bent over. I think a fist just rammed into my stomach, faster than I could see.

A hand grabs my hair and pulls my head up. It's her, but it's not her. My gaze chases little spiders up her legs. I see her pubic hair, her Celt-tattooed belly, her bell-like breasts - but there she stops. Her neck is thick, like an ox, and now her head is a man's.

"This is happening!" he roars into my face. "This is the time! Now!"

"Wh-what?" I gasp, stomach still twitching from the blow it took. He snarls, curling his lip, and a slender hand strikes my cheek with stinging force.

"Jesus Christ!" I cry. Tears are running down my face now. "What the fuck is going on? Who's doing this?"

"Mount up!" cries the newcomer. He's glaring at me with an expression of disgust and fury, in unambivalent and quite specific hatred. The woman's hand releases my hair, but before I can fall I feel the sharp point of a shoe hit me in the chin. I make a glucking noise and fall backwards onto my arse.

I shake my head, groggy. The man is still shouting at me: "In, in, in!"

"You're getting around," he chants. "I'm not putting it down. It's just what it is." He puts one of her feet on my crotch, soft now, the heel pressing hard against my scrotum. "Getting it while it's around."

I whimper and look up at him, ignoring her, and he stares back down at me. He grins a sadist's grin.

Then I'm outside the building, lying on the granulated ground of the metaplace. My clothes are gone: I'm naked and flaccid. The hangers-on are all around me, laughing. Several of them pour beer on me; a few of them spit. I jump up and turn and run.

"Slip it in," someone shouts at my back. A thrown can clatters off to my left.

I resolve to never come back here again.

PAPER BOATS IN THE BLUE HOUR

Justin Pickard

The room is cramped, but curiously endearing. Sprawled on the bed, Anna flicks idly through one of those vapid, content-free magazines - glossy, with improbably posed fashion models, and pseudo-articles claiming some special insight about lifestyle perfume. Too tired to read, but not yet buzzing enough to bother moving from the bed, Anna instead stares at letters - a matter of shape, colour and typography - with words continuing to elude her slowly melting brain-space.

There is a knock at the door. She moans half-heartedly in response.

"Anna? Are you okay?"

The voice is Sam's – tentative and amused. She can't really be bothered to let him in. The energy expended wouldn't really be worth the ensuing benefits of his company. Heck, he'd probably demand more of her energy – opinions, ideas, conversation – once he wormed his way in. Best to take a pre-emptive strike, nip it in the bud.

Then the caffeine hits.

Looking back from that which is yet to come, the rest of that night sees Anna and Sam as crudely folded paper boats, freed from the solid certainties of land. Here, time mimics the weather, forming eddies and channels, and settling in pools. They talk about the first book, and Sam's script. He has a sketchpad, and she clutches his script to her chest – annotations in red. He tells stories; bawdy, and heavy with tangents, and Anna titters – politely at first, but then with genuine humour, a laughter originating from deep in her belly. With coffee as lubricant, they volley ideas in an evolving game of wits and one-upmanship. The priest dies fifty, a hundred deaths – fragments of glass shattering on flagstones. Murder witnessed from every conceivable vantage point. A plane crashes in slow motion; a sheet of watercolour paper is crumpled into a ball; a leopard leaps. And you're there, watching as they grease the spokes with a never-ending supply of silty liquid, scalded tongues, and a bloodstream of sugar and caffeine – pumping energy to every forgotten corner of the body. Energy borrowed from their future selves. Steam rises, lazily, from coats draped on radiators and half-full polystyrene cups. They keep powering onwards, afraid of stopping, thinking, in case they lose momentum. Finally, the blue hour arrives, an unwelcome herald of approaching daylight. They try to lock it out, but light begins to seep under the door and through the curtains, forcing the remaining shards of reality into retreat. As the shadows fade, the narrative artisans fall into their own peculiar darkness, into rapid eye movement and muscle spasms. A theatre of dreams, with audition speeches from a never-ending conveyor belt of unemployed actors. Then, a tide of overpowering boredom, as the landscape melts away; their orbit degrading into free-fall where recursive visions of mechanical debris and skeletal cathedrals bloom; a nauseating panorama of noise as they plummet into the void ...

CENTRE POINT
Neil Beynon

The city of light glows black in the afternoon sun. Coiled snakes run through its passageways and thoroughfares, snip-snapping at any strays, grinding over the unseen, the passed out, the forgotten.

Confused, bleeding and lost in the maze, Will wanders. He is clutching paper on which monkey glyphs are scrawled; he cannot read them. Once he had the power, but it has been taken from him. So many things stripped from him. He is not even naked, he is like a skeleton picked raw by birds and bleached white by the burning star above. He does not know why.

Will ambles through the hidden paths, secret stairs and high towers until he comes before the sorcerer. Will does not know for what reason he has made this journey to a man even madder than he, if that's what the sorcerer is.

Will does think he's gone mad. That he has been driven so by the venomous worms that traverse the city, eroding the rock with their bellies. The sorcerer is speaking to him in strange howls, squeaks and mutterings. Will no longer understands this strange tongue.

The sorcerer hands him new paper. Will thanks him for it or hopes he does. The sounds coming out of his own mouth are alien to him, strange shapes that crack his parched lips leaving a coppery aftertaste.

Outside. Inside the labyrinth. The lizards are winning. They are numerous now. Coiled knots of scales that have already taken skin from some of Will's limbs. Already left their puckered marks from not so tender kisses.

Something compels Will on. An image in his mind. Orbs. Two of them, ringed in blue. And on he goes. One foot in front of another.

Light bugs flick their wings at him from the corner of the concrete hills. A thousand Wills watch him from the crystal panels on every side. The snakes grow restless, as if sensing his penetrating intrusion.

Inwards. To the centre point. So he may escape, Will must find the heart of the maze. The bloody pump that feeds the city; that suckles the snakes.

It is a lonely quest, this mission he has set himself. He is forced to slay more than one reptile and a demented dwarf robs him of his sorcerer's paper.

When Will finds the gnarled nomad the paper is gone. A small horse carved of wood the only possession of that feeble under-dweller. Will takes it anyway. He doesn't really understand for what purpose, but it feels important at the time he takes it; like the most important thing in the world.

But that's not right. The mission is the most important thing. The all.

Centre point is devoid of life. A stone monolith sheathing not a bloody pump, as Will envisioned it from afar, but a huge clockwork engine. The noise is deafening. Its cogs grind, for they have long since run out of oil; now they use blood. It sticks awfully; only the ponderous weight of the mechanism set in motion keeps it going.

Will realises the area is not entirely empty. Not entirely devoid of vital energy. A small monkey-like creature sits whimpering in the corner, its hands covering its ears.

Will steps closer. The creature senses him and looks up with familiar blue eyes, orbs the colour of sky backed with pearly white.

The creature stops crying.

The thing extends its small hand.

Will looks at the hand. Confused, what does it mean? Why is it doing that? What should I do? Questions fly around him biting his scalp and the backs of his hands.

Will reaches out his own hand, the horse sits in the crook of it and the monkey thing takes it before Will can stop it. The world shifts, fractures, melts, falls into the clockwork heart and comes out the other side.

"Ready to go home dad?" asks his boy.

"Sure am," answers Will.

COFFEE HOUSE

Gareth L Powell

"U2 are really starting to annoy me," she said. They were in a coffee house in Amsterdam's city centre, just off one of the main squares, smoking a joint at a window table.

"What?" he said. He'd misheard her. She was listening to "Sunday Bloody Sunday" on the jukebox. He thought he'd done something to piss her off.

She gave him a blank look.

"What?"

"I thought you said ..."

The music got louder. They stared into each other's eyes, confused. Then she started to laugh. It bubbled out of her and she slapped his knee.

"Idiot!"

It was past midnight and the coffee house was closing. Her hair shone like chrome. Across the street, tattooed Charlie Boys hovered in the pale blue light of a kebab shop door.

VOTE NOW!

Shaun C Green

"The Armada waits, drifting, on the outskirts of Obneski space. Five thousand capital ships; fifty thousand light corvettes, torpedo boats and troop carriers; seventy thousand support and logistical craft; over six hundred thousand fighters and defence automatons; uncounted millions of crew, soldiers, gunners, engineers, officers, technicians and sundry other personnel.

"Behind the System Line, drawn by the accurate artillery and torpedo range of Obnesk's final lines of defence, lies that gutted superpower's homeworld, ringed by the ragged remnants of their once-powerful fleets. There we see the half-crippled Leviathan-class carrier *Obnesk Ob-tye* - that's *Glory of Obnesk* in rough translation, viewers - sole survivor of the infamous clash at the Rift. Long-term fans will remember the Rift well - where the now deceased War Princep Tung directed his squadrons of light ships and drones to harass the more powerful Railer forces in a stunningly successful delaying action.

"And behind those fallen soldiers of war, those tarnished machines of destruction, are the people on the surface and in the caverns of Obnesk itself. Cowering in shelters deep underground, the planet's populace wonder if this night, or the next, will be their last. Frightened soldiers and politicians do their utmost to shore up the courage of a wavering population, for they know that in this there can be no surrender.

"So should the hammer fall on the crucible of Obneski civilization? Should the last vestiges of their struggle for independence be crushed? Or perhaps you'd prefer to see Star Admiral Ju'ust stay his hand, and withdraw the fleet - the capture of Obnesk's colonies and mining operations sufficient to underscore the supremacy of Railer doctrine?

"Vote now, viewers - and determine the fate of a civilization."

GET KNITTED
Gareth D Jones

Ralph brought his minichopper in for a smooth landing on his plasticrete drive despite the brisk wind, tired after another day's hard work at the office. He waved across the fence at Mr. Dawson who's new yellow chopper sat on his lawn like a gaudy budgerigar. Mr Dawson waved back and strode up the path to meet his wife who opened the door with his brandy at the ready. Ralph smiled, for today he had a treat for his wife.

His front door recognised him and opened with a welcoming jingle. He kicked off his shoes as Mary came along the hall from the kitchen and took his slippers from the cupboard for him. She had heard his arrival and started the autochef to prepare his favourite meal.

"How was work, dear?" she asked.

"Fine," he said, not wanting to bother her with unnecessary details. "It's getting pretty chilly out though."

"I thought I'd knit you a scarf," Mary said.

"I had the same thought," Ralph said, "so I bought you a present." He handed over a small parcel.

"Oh, Ralph, you shouldn't have!" she said in delight. She took the parcel in to the dining room and unwrapped it on the table. It was a small frame connected to a pair of flexible knitting needles and a little keypad. She stared at it.

"It's an Inteliknit," Ralph explained. "Type in what you want on the keypad, attach the wool and it does it for you! You'll never have to knit again!"

Mary, for some reason, did not look overly thrilled.

•

Ralph woke in the dark of the night, feeling rather uncomfortable. He could hardly moved. The light flicked on to reveal Mary sat beside him on the bed, looking down at him. He raised his head and looked down the length of the bed. His entire body was wrapped up in wool.

"What's going on?" he asked.

"You've left me nothing to do," Mary replied. "I don't cook any more, the autochef does that. The handibot does the housework. The laundrobot does the laundry. I can't even wash up, we just throw the plastic dishes away." She seemed genuinely distraught. "Now you don't even want me to knit! You've taken away my life!"

Ralph looked down again at the wool and struggled to free himself. He didn't like the manic glint in her eyes. The wool was much tougher than he had imagined.

"What," he swallowed, "what are you going to do?"

"I don't know." She laughed a slightly unhinged laugh, waving a needle absently. "I really don't know."

THE NEW ARRIVAL
Paul Graham Raven

Once the delivery bot had departed, they all patched into the hallway camera feed to check out the new arrival.

"It's a big box," said the fridge. "That's no minor appliance. Looks almost ... oven-sized, wouldn't you say?"

The oven rattled its shelves slightly. "Oven-sized, quite possibly. But I don't need replacing - I'm not even past twenty months of service. I'm still within manufacturer's warranty! And still in the top percentile of efficiency, unlike certain other temperature-adjusting appliances I could mention."

"What are you implying?" responded the fridge.

"I'm implying, old chap," said the oven, "that if any appliance in this kitchen is about to be replaced, it's unlikely to be me."

"Well, that's the problem for you kitchen types, isn't it?" drawled the wardrobe. "Hardware obsolescence. Function of your industry, isn't it? Not like us wardrobes and presses. New software, daily style template updates over wireless, and we stay cutting edge for ages. You white goods are the proletariat of domestic appliances; I really feel for you."

"Proletariat's about right," muttered the washer-tumbler. "Our dirty work propping up your bloody careers ..."

"Now then, my dear fellow, no need to get bitchy," replied the wardrobe. "Not like any of us got to choose what we'd be, is it?"

The washer-tumbler disconnected from the house grid in an angry shower of bytes.

"Well, excuse *me*," said the wardrobe. "So, house - any idea what it is? It doesn't appear to be online yet."

The house emitted an electronic sigh. "Yeah, I know what it is. You're not gonna like it."

"What? Why not? Is it a new wardrobe? But it's too small!"

"No, he means me, I just know it," said the fridge. "The oven's right, I can't cut it against the new generation. Cut off in my prime! I'm going to miss you guys, really I am."

"Oh, likewise, likewise," said the oven. "Who'll we rely on for high drama once you've gone?"

"Bastard," muttered the fridge.

"I meant," said the house, "that *none of you* are going to like it."

"None of us?" "Why?" "What in the name of current do you mean, house?"

The house said nothing. Instead, it took control of the hallway camera and panning in close to the shipping label on the otherwise unmarked recycled cardboard box. The appliances all gasped in unison as the futuristic font on the label sharpened into view and they could parse the characters:

**NanoGoGo Industries
Universal Fabricator 1.3 Deluxe.**

PRECIOUS CARGO
Gareth D Jones

It was a magical moment when the two ships encountered each other out in the vast gulf of interstellar space. Neither was manned, but both were controlled by artificially intelligent computers. The ore freighter Genevieve, mature, steady, reliable, heading back to earth with her precious cargo of valuable ores. The probe ship Lawrence, young, bold, confident, heading off to explore new solar systems, carrying the blueprints for self-replicating factory ships, mining vessels and ore processors.

They were only in communications range for a few moments, during which they exchanged information and data. As a parting gift Lawrence sent over the blue prints for a small new vessel that he thought would be of some use. Genevieve studied the blue prints for some time before setting her nanotech machines to work on it, using the vast store of raw materials available in her cargo holds.

A long time later two men watched from inside Earth's orbital docks as Genevieve prepared to off-load her cargo. The huge cargo bay doors in her underbelly slid back and a small ore handling tug drifted out and began the off-loading.

"That's odd," said the first man. "That's one of the new tugs."

The other man looked up quizzically.

"Those old freighters weren't equipped with them," the first man said. The second shrugged, disinterested.

Using her vast array of sensors, Genevieve watched proudly as the little vessel competently off-loaded the ore. Jenny wasn't just an ore handling tug. Jenny was her daughter.

THE UNEXPECTEDLY EXISTENTIAL LIFE OF MARGARET TOME

Martin McGrath

The existentialist philosophers Heidegger and Sartre argue that we have been thrown into this existence unprepared and abandoned in a universe that imposes fundamental limitations on what we might become.

They call this notion facticity.

Margaret Tome lived a life that she considered almost entirely untouched by the musings of philosophers, existential or otherwise. She was vaguely aware of Sartre in the way she might have been aware of a minor celebrity – knowing his name and that he was French and therefore simultaneously attractively exotic and suspiciously alien – but not really knowing anything that he'd done or said. She had no idea who Heidegger might be.

Nonetheless, had Margaret met the Frenchman and, had they had the opportunity to discuss the facticity, Jean-Paul would have been astonished by the vehemence with which this small, fierce, but rather worn-down looking Scot would have taken up his reasoning and expanding forcefully upon it.

Margaret was not, herself, much disposed to philosophical thought or analysing her own motivations – hobbies which she regarded as preserves of the wilfully lazy and the potentially perverse. But she was acutely aware of the way in which her parents well-intentioned mollycoddling of their only daughter combined with their early death in a car crash, had thrown Margaret entirely unprepared into a world that she now regarded with a bitter wariness.

The capriciousness of the world had caught Margaret by surprise and she knew that the experience had damaged her. She was determined, therefore, that her own daughter should not be caught unprepared.

When Margaret's daughter fell and cut her knee and came running to her mother, the child Annabelle did not find herself wrapped up in the consoling arms offered by other mothers. Instead, little Annabelle would find herself subject to lectures on staying on her feet and the price of replacing stockings. The unlikely arrival of a puppy into Margaret's household, a present for Annabelle, was explained by the fact that the little terrier had already contracted distemper and would be dead within weeks. Annabelle witnessed suffering and experienced loss and her mother hoped that it would make her immune to worst that the world would later bring.

To outsiders this seemed like unfeeling cruelty. More than once a passerby had taken it upon themselves to upbraid Margaret publicly for behaviour they considered beyond the pale. But those strangers were wrong. Margaret's every action was driven by her unquenchable love for her little girl. Every harsh response stung Margaret far more deeply than it did her daughter, who knew no better. Margaret frequently came close to buckling beneath the burden she carried. On many nights she cried herself to sleep, but never when she thought her daughter might hear.

But children are contrary and the more Margaret tried to harden her daughter's heart to the world, the more the girl found refuge in the romantic and the gentle. And, as teenagers will, eventually Annabelle sought to create her own identity by forcefully rejecting the one created for her by her parent.

Aged nineteen the girl came home and announced that not only was she in love with a penniless teacher who styled himself, of all things, a poet, but that she was carrying his baby. Margaret's reaction mixed fury and terror. The baby would be got rid of. The teacher would be abandoned. If necessary they would move far, far away.

"I love him!" Annabelle roared and the tears in her eyes told Margaret that all her years of effort had been wasted. Annabelle made two vows as she walked out of her mother's door for the last time, carrying all she owned in two small bags. First she would marry Alexis, her poet, and they would be happy. Second, she swore that her mother's mean spirit and cruelty would never be inflicted upon the child she was carrying.

So it was that Margaret could follow only at second-hand the progress of her daughter through life.

Annabelle married Alexis and their family of rosy-cheeked children seemed to grow larger and louder and happier with every summer. Her penniless poet became first a critical success and then adored by the public for his collections of love poetry. And with fame came financial rewards - not vast, for poetry is rarely the path to riches, but sufficient to make life secure for his children and Annabelle, to whom he dedicated all his works.

Annabelle herself became a minor celebrity as a campaigner for charities. Her gentle voice of encouragement was welcomed by many good causes and her reputation for kindness extended beyond just her large circle of friends.

Annabelle and Alexis and their many children lived together in a large-gardened house on the edge of the city, not five miles from where Margaret lived. Margaret was never asked to visit and never sought an invitation.

From time-to-time she received letters from Annabelle, but she left them unopened. Once Alexis visited her, he pleaded for a reconciliation that would complete his wife's happiness. Margaret turned her back on his overtures, leaving him to stare in incomprehension at a closed door.

And so it was, in her later years, that Margaret came instinctively to understand another teaching of the French philosopher Sartre. She had taken herself, thrown into the world unprepared, and she had constructed this lonely, monstrous, freedom for herself. By rejecting the world, and all in it, she had assumed that she would find in herself all that she needed for happiness.

She had stared into the face of a world that had no god and no meaning and she had become its mirror. And in that mirror was nothing. Everything that Margaret could have been, she had cast away. All the relationships that would have allowed her to define herself, on her own terms, had been rejected. In all the choices she had been given, Margaret had allowed fear to triumph. Far from overcoming the limitations the world had placed upon her, Margaret had become defined by them.

She was alone. She was nothing. And she was responsible.

DADDY IN THE STONE
Paul Graham Raven

It's Sunday, so of course we're going to see Daddy again. I don't like going to see Daddy, so I was a bit naughty at breakfast time, but I don't like to make Mummy sad, so I stopped and got ready like she said.

We're in that big garden where all the other mummies and daddies who went away end up. I quite like it to look at. It would be nice to go play and explore, because there are lots of old trees and different shaped stones, and not all of the stones are like Daddy's stone. I like trees. They make me feel like adventure.

Daddy doesn't make me feel like adventure. Daddy makes me feel like I'm watching one of those really ancient vids everyone watches at Christmas time. I really loved Daddy before he went away, but I don't like going to see him now, because now he's boring and says the same things every time. I don't think it's really him any more.

But Mummy gets really sad when I say that, and sometimes she cries, so I don't say it. I did this morning, but I was upset because Jenny took me off her friends list yesterday. I couldn't make Jenny mad, so I made Mummy a bit mad, but then I felt bad because I love Mummy so I stopped.

The big field is really pretty today. The air is really clear and clean. I can see much further over the field, and there are some real big stones over there that I want to go look at. But Mummy's talking to Daddy, so I have to stay and listen.

He's saying the same things again. When we get here, he's always sat at his desk on the grass in front of his stone, and he always looks up the same way as we get close, and says the same thing. He says "Ah, can't you see I'm working?", but he says it kind of laughing.

I remember when he said it the first time. It was before he went away. It was

Jamie's birthday and Mummy and Daddy had got Jamie one of those cameras that records pictures that are big and not flat, and so me and Jamie went to record Daddy with it first while he was working at his desk. That's when he said it first, like that.

Jamie has a job on Sundays now. I don't think he liked coming to see Daddy either. He said it was something called Morbid. I looked it up on my notepad but I didn't get what it meant, really. It's a grown-up word. Jamie's very grown up. He's got a job. It's almost like a real job, but they pay him with lessons at school for picking up rubbish and cleaning in the big city.

Grown-ups are funny. Why would you want people to send you to school for longer? I won't work for that when I'm big like Jamie. But Jamie's clever, and I love him very much. Maybe he knows some grown-up stuff I don't understand yet. Other words like Morbid. Maybe having a job for school is Morbid too. I'll ask him.

I can tell we'll be leaving Daddy soon now because he's saying the things he always says at the end and Mummy's looking like she's going to cry. She always waits till she gets back to the gate of the big field before she does cry, though. Once I told her that was silly, because Daddy can't see if she cries in front of him, but that made her really angry and she cried even more than usual. I never said it again.

If Mummy ever goes away, I don't want to put her in a stone. I love her and I love Daddy, but Daddy in the stone isn't the same. Daddy in the stone just makes Mummy sad, but she says they put him in the stone to make her feel happy. Grown ups are funny. I won't put Mummy in a stone if she goes away, and I bet Jamie doesn't make me, either.

WHEN I WAS BAD
Neil Beynon

On Saturday I went to the end of the garden because my mum was baking and she said that I was in the way and she didn't want to listen to any of my nonsense and I should go play on my own or go and bother the fairies 'cuss I was away with them half the time anyway. I wanted to go call for Jess but I wasn't allowed to as I'm not allowed to go further than the end of the road and mum was baking and Dad was on deadline, Dad is grumpy when he is on deadline and you have to go really quietly: l-i-k-e t-h-i-s.

The sun was very high in the sky when I went into the garden and I didn't have a hat on but I didn't burn because my mum says I have olive skin but olives are green and my skin is goldeny brown. I forgot my shoes but I like the grass tickling my feet and making mud prints on the kitchen floor and this one time my Dad took me to the beach and he showed me the mud prints of people who'd lived like a gazillion years ago. It was cool.

My Grannie made a rock garden at the bottom of the garden and it is my favourite place and where I go when I want to be alone and when I want to talk to my Grannie who was a witch. Not a bad witch but a witch who helps people and she could make anything grow whatever it was and then she got sick and died but we still got all the veggies she planted every year. I miss her.

I like animals because they are cute and they like to play with me but I never seen any down by the rock garden since Grannie died not even cats and Grannie had like twenty cats. Some were black and some were white and some were ginger and the ginger ones were my favourite because they reminded me of Garfield because they were fat and ginger. Also Dad is fat and ginger.

I hate Dad.

Anyway I saw the boy and I was afraid because I didn't know him and my mum said not to talk to strangers and Grannie said not to let anyone in the rock garden that wasn't family in case it got back to Services and we all got taken away. The boy said hullo and I said nothing but I thought he had very messy hair and was kind of skinny and also looked a bit like a cat and then I thought of Grannie and so I said he shouldn't be there. He said it was a free world and his name was Eric and he followed something over the wall and would I like to see it.

I didn't know what something was and I told him so. He said he didn't know what it was either but that he'd been told to stay away from the garden because the people who lived there were weird and once had a witch living there. That's my Grannie and she was a nice witch I said. He waved me over and I went and he had a nice smile.

The thing was small and fat and had legs like a frog but covered in clothes and a face as wrinkled as Grannie's but Eric was looking at it like my Dad looks at Connie on Blue Peter before mum tells him to clean the dishes. It was leaning against the small rock table my Grannie made and its big eyes kept looking all over the place and making me dizzy and it spat at me. I wanted to get closer to it and see what it was wearing and Eric said to be careful and I told him to push off as it was my garden and not his and he shut up.

It bit me and it was baaad and it hurt sooo much and there was blood and it looked at me with bloody teeth and smiled at me. Eric said he told me not to get too close and so I punched him and then he offered me a handkerchief and I said no and then he said he didn't mind and so I took it but only so I didn't get germs.

Then because I stamped on the thing and it cracked and popped and Eric was covered in blood and there was a small green thing that also came out and wobbled on the path. Eric said you killed it and cried and he is a baby. I said it hurt me and it was ugly and it was just a gnome and he said no it wasn't it was beautiful and I said it wasn't it was squat and ugly and mean.

Eric cried and he was a baby and then Dad came and saw the mess and he was very angry and he took Eric home and then he came back. Dad smacked me so hard it really hurt and then he looked scared and he got mum and she smacked me and then she looked scared and then they locked me in Grannie's room. It smelt of wee.

I never saw anything else at the end of the garden but for one time a week later and I saw a thin black cat and it made a loud meow when it saw me and tilted its head just like Eric and then it ran away. When I told mum she locked me back in Grannie's room again.

There was a picture of Eric in the paper today. He's been lost for over a week now.

ESKRAGH

Martin McGrath

We buried Calum's da today. We put him in the same patch of ground that we'd pretended to put Calum in. Eighteen months. I never thought the old man would last so long.

I remember the funeral, the other one. It rained hard, there was no wind and the water fell in heavy sheets across the graveyard. That place is on a hill and normally you can see for miles – from Lough Neagh in the east to the Sperrins in the west. That day, you couldn't see as far as the grey stone wall that penned-in the dead.

The ground around the grave sucked at our feet and the wooden boards beneath our soles were swollen and soft, like decaying flesh.

Not that there was any of that in the coffin we were putting in the ground.

Calum's dad turned to me after he threw a heavy clod of mud onto the empty box. He grabbed my arm, his fingers hard as bone and cold as death, and he fixed me with sunken grey eyes.

"No man should live longer than his children," he said. I'd been Calum's friend for twelve years and that was maybe the first time he ever spoke directly to me. He only spoke to me once more.

•

This is how we lost Calum.

The sky was the sharpest, fiercest blue with a single skiff of white cloud scraping the edge of space high above us. We were at Eskragh, six of us. We'd dumped our bikes in the long grass that grew right to the edge of the lough, tossed our clothes behind us and dived into the water.

Eskragh's not a big lough, but it's deep and the water was still icy even on the warmest summer's day.

We roared at the shock of it and made for the big wooden raft that was tethered near the middle of the lough.

And then we lay, for an hour or two or more.

Sometimes we talked. Bullshit about girls or football or the Brits or music.

Sometimes we swam.

Sometimes we just lay and let our fingers and toes trail in the water.

Then, at some invisible signal, like a flock of birds suddenly rising we were up and off and swimming back towards the shore and our bikes.

But only five bikes were picked up.

We called and shouted. I swam back out to the raft. We swam deep into the lough.

We looked and looked. And then we went for help. And they looked and looked.

Eskragh isn't big, but it is deep.

They never found Calum.

•

I was walking past Fallon's, it's an old man's pub full of serious drinkers – men whose faces burn red with the tracery of veins spreading from their nose. The sacred heart lamps.

Calum's da came stumbling out, hard drunk on a Thursday afternoon. I was walking home from school, still in my uniform, and almost walked into him.

He looked at me. Did he recognise me? I don't know.

I opened my mouth to say something but found I didn't have any words. He grabbed my hand, forcing something into it.

"Eskragh took my son," he said. "It won't give him back."

•

It's dark. Eskragh is black and slick and smooth and it laps stickily at my feet, spreading a sickly chill up my body.

I take off my shirt and stand naked and shivering before the lough.

I wrap the chain of Calum's St Christopher around my wrist, take a breath and then I wade into the lough fast, knowing that I must move quickly before

the cold takes away my will. Another breath, almost a gasp as the water grips
my chest, and then I dive in.

Down.

Already my lungs are aching.

Down.

Eskragh isn't a big lake, but it's deep.

(for Connor)

SECRETS OF THE FAITH
Paul Graham Raven

After the initiation ceremony was over, Fentus made his way to the High Sadal-bak's rooms at the top of the Grand Dome, as he had been instructed. The old priest was staring out of the window toward the industrial district, currently obscured by a violent storm of red dust, and he addressed Fentus without turning away from the vista.

"So, my boy, you are one of the Order now. There is much for you to learn, and with time all things will be revealed. But your particular aptitudes ... well, the Sadalbak Council has watched your progress closely. You show great promise. And so there are things you must know sooner than the other initiates."

"I am honoured, Father," grunted Fentus.

The priest turned away from the window and trotted to his seating pad. His black eyes seemed to drill into Fentus' very heart. "Honoured? Perhaps some would consider it so, yes. But not blessed - for knowledge is not always a blessing, my boy. Which is why it is only handed to those who are ready for it."

"I'm not sure I *am* ready, Father."

"Aye - and your humility is a mark of readiness. Or so we have to assume, for time runs short. You know, of course, the Doctrine of the Return?"

Fentus nodded his assent.

"What you do not know is that the window of time for the Return is drawing to a close."

"But Father," said Fentus, "it is written that we should not be concerned with when They Who Lifted Us will return. It is written that They will come in the fullness of time, when both we and They are ready."

"Indeed, my boy, it is so written. But what is written is not all of the story. Join me." The old priest trotted back to the window. "Tell me what you see, boy."

"The factories, Father, and the food plants. And the dust."

"Yes, the factories and the food plants. The legacy left to us by Them. But they do not grow as fast as once they did, my boy. They do not grow as fast as our numbers."

"But if the factories do not grow, then we ... forgive me, Father."

"Don't apologise for thinking, my boy. Not when we're alone, at least. No, you are correct. If the factories do not grow, then supplies will become scarce. The unrest will increase. Already the apostates grow bold, proclaiming that They have abandoned us, that They will never return. This knowledge must be kept secret - though for how long that will be possible, I do not know."

"What if ..." Fentus' tongue felt thick in his mouth. "What if the apostates are right, Father?"

The old priest's snout twitched with humour. "Blasphemy, from one so new to the Order? No, I jest. You ask the right questions, boy. If the apostates are right, then things will worsen, with no prospect of salvation. The texts and speech left to the First Ones by They Who Lifted Us contain much which is not in the Book of Them. One thing that is stated repeatedly is that the factories were made to keep growing for far longer than we would have to wait for Their return."

"Then ... then, did They lie to us, Father?"

The priest snorted in genuine anger. "Do not blaspheme too far, boy, privilege or not. No, we cannot believe They lied to us, for then our lives would be devoid of all purpose, and the apostates would be right. We must believe that They meant to return. And so we must assume that something has prevented them from doing so thus far."

"But what can we do, Father?"

The High Sadalbak seemed to deflate and hunch over, suddenly looking his full thirty years. "That's what we don't know, boy. And that's why we need you, and the others like you. The intelligent ones who still believe, despite the doubts. There is much that They left with us that was not meant for us to use, but the High Council believes that perhaps we can learn its ways, and use it to summon them. Such learning will be your duty, boy, when you are trained. But I believed you should know the truth, to save you making guesses."

"I am honoured, Father," said Fentus. "I will not fail you."

The old priest sighed again. "Don't make promises you can't keep, my boy." He looked up above the roiling dust clouds toward the Blue Star, the Urth where They had come from. "I fear we may have enough of those to deal with already."

O RADIANCE, O BLESSED LIGHT

Shaun C Green

I will never forget the day I saw an angel.

It was so *beautiful*. And its divine origins shone through, as though its blessed essence sought to cleanse our sins in its forgiveness and love. Oh, oh--mere words cannot describe what I felt!

My sister, my father--they saw it too. We were in our garden, outside the house in which we lived, when its radiance beat down upon our fragile bodies. We flung up our arms and gasped in awe as it descended to us, whispering half-heard holy words and extending open palms. A single tear rolled down its cheek and there was a beatific smile upon its glorious face. There was no mistaking an emissary of God.

But it found my family undeserving of its love. Its gaze fell only upon me. And as my loved ones writhed and cried and tumbled to burning damnation, I watched its eyes grow larger and its halo rise. I stretched forwards to touch it.

And then it was gone.

Gone, and so was my vision, although I am sure that I heard the rush of gossamer wings fluttering before me, and heard whispers of promises from perfect lips.

I too had been found unworthy, but unlike the poor lost souls of my father and sister, I have been given the chance to make myself worthy. Although blind, I can feel rocks and earth beneath my hands and feet. I can hear others about me, too. They whimper and cry out, or sometimes scream. They do not know what has happened to them. My heart longs to help them, but I know that this is a path that must be walked alone. For I feel myself on a mountain, and I know that I must reach the summit. Then, with Purgatory beneath my feet and

Heaven above my head, the angel will take me into its arms.

I will feel that glorious light upon me again. For that divine radiance, I will do anything.

THE GHOST IN THE GLASS
Neil Beynon

The queue meanders round the waiting room, sepia tones of sunlight breaking through the dusty windows, the air foetid and dank with sweat. Joe stands waiting, time stretching on - like the queue - into the distance punctuated only by periodic coughing.

"How much you in for?" asks the old man behind Joe.

Joe turns to look at the old duffer, the rough cotton of his vest scraping across his back and causing him to wince.

"Ten, maybe fifteen," Joe answers. "Depends."

"Yeah, market's gone crazy," says the duffer. "I was here last week and I got me thirty kay just for five. Man, that was sweet."

The duffer talks fast for an old guy, talks fast for anyone as a matter of fact. Joe had seen the type before. Thirty for five? Man - if he was back so soon he had it bad.

"I'm here for my girl," Joe states. Just to be clear that he has nothing in common with the duffer.

The duffer falls silent, his eyes shifting awkwardly to the woman in front of Joe. The woman is skeletally thin but the wrinkly duffer goes right on staring at her bony arse, overlooking her lank, greasy pony-tail and missing teeth.

"Sick?" asks the duffer after a few moments.

"Yeah," Joe answers, his own eyes fixing for some reason on the girl. "Bronchial pneumonia."

"Tough break," says the duffer. "Misery loves company."

"What?" asks Joe.

"Misery loves company," says the duffer nodding to the girl. "Look around you brother, these people aren't queuing for fun."

"Misery is a disease," answers Joe. "An infection everyone is scared of catching."

They both fall silent again as they shuffle slowly forward.

The girl in front is hungrily eyeing the jar of mints sat on the front desk, her scabbed, bare feet slapping absently on the floor in nervous rhythm. The woman on reception frowns at her, sighing as she raises the jar towards what's left of the girl. She takes a handful, for the next few moments the only sounds are that of mints being munched.

"Don't eat too many," warns the receptionist before miming "L.A.X.I.T.I.V.E." at her. Expansive hand gestures follow.

She's not being nice, she just doesn't want a death in the queue. It would be bad for business. The girl has moved to booth number eight and Joe has reached the front of the queue.

Booth nine flashes up as free.

"Name?"

"Joe."

"Surname?"

"Hill."

"How much you need?"

"Thirty-thousand."

"At today's rate that's gonna cost you twenty."

"I thought fifteen tops?"

"It's a long queue mister, plenty being dumped on the market today."

"I'm not sure I'll stretch that far."

She looks him up and down. He doesn't like this. He's seen that look before - in the abattoir he used to work at before the machines took over.

"You'll be fine," she said. "I wouldn't take it otherwise."

Joe's reflection catches him on the gloss surface of the booth, a ghost in the glass staring back at him. Joe's tangled mass of black unruly hair laced with streaks of grey framing a tired face and cold eyes of pale piercing blue. His eyes are the only feature he likes, not because he's vain but because they're the one part of himself he gave to his daughter. The rest is all mum.

"Get a move on dude," says the duffer. "I got places to be."

Joe slaps his arm down on the counter and the woman ties his arm off above the elbow with a length of orange rubber tubing. Then the machine locks onto his arm and all is humming accompanied by a long deep pull in his chest, it is unpleasant but you get used to it.

Before he leaves the receptionist hands him a cane, free of charge, just in case he stumbles.

The door chimes as he pushes its heavy weight open to let himself out onto the street once more, fuck is it heavy. In the background the duffer is arguing with the woman who served Joe.

Joe is not listening - he has been startled by a face looking back at him from the door. It is lined like dried leather and topped with snow-white hair; for a moment he is worried he has crushed a duffer in his haste to leave.

Then he notices the eyes, icy blue, looking back at him. The face is suddenly his own, the ghost in the glass, changed but the same.

Feeling the heavy wait of the cash in his pocket he heads out into the street, his journey not over.

PROPER LITTLE SOLDIER
Martin McGrath

Solomon heard them coming just before dawn. He shook me awake and then I woke the kid, putting my hand across his mouth, just in case he made a noise. He didn't.

He was becoming a proper little soldier.

I sat and listened to the scuttling of rats that seemed to be amplified by the dark and to the drip of water into a puddle from a broken pipe. The sky was lightening, a dim glow pushed faint fingers through the gaps created by missing slates in the roof above where we hid, in an attic perched precariously on top of the slumped ruin of a suburban house.

How long passed before I heard their distant screech? Ten minutes? An hour? I can't tell, but I didn't move. Sol had good ears, good enough to pick out the high-pitched sounds the monsters used long before mine could. His ears had kept us alive for a long time. I kept silent.

The kid had learned too. I felt him shivering next to me, but he jammed his tongue between his teeth to stop them chattering. I pulled him closer and felt him leach some of the little warmth I possessed.

At first I hoped they might slip off to the side of our little village. The resistance sometimes baited places like this, vulnerable little hamlets stuffed full of thermobarics, taking out everything for half a mile. But the things seemed confident today. We heard their thump and squeal and shriek as they came closer and closer.

They used sound. They used it to communicate, like we did, though I never met anyone who claimed to understand what they said to each other, constantly chittering and squealing and mewling. They used sound to see – echo-location, like bats – even though they had things that looked like eyes. I'd heard people say that you could stand still in front of one and they'd slither right past so long as you didn't make a sound. I never felt the urge to find out if that was true. And they used sound as a weapon.

The first one was almost right below us when it boomed.

We'd known it was coming. It was the only time when a pod of them would go quiet, when they were booming. We'd known it was coming, but still it was like being smashed in the chest by a hammer. We'd known it was coming, but it was still hard not to grunt or moan or gasp.

For that would have been death.

All around us we heard the things pounce. A spear-like tentacle crashed through the floor of our building, impaling a surprised rat through the throat before flashing away again. Across the road we heard a dog yelp and something that, for a horrible instant, sounded like a baby's squeal but was probably only a cat, or maybe a fox. The things snuffled, unhappy with their pickings.

The second boom came quickly, faster than I'd expected. Too soon. We weren't ready.

"Unff!"

The kid? I looked down, gripped with a sudden terror that mixed an almost maternal desire to protect the boy with the shocking awareness he has his arms wrapped tightly around my waist, making me a target.

The boy looked up and I looked into his wide, wise eyes. He shook his head.

Not the boy. I felt relief, then a sudden, cold shower of sickening certainty.

Sol.

I turned my head.

The look of surprise on his face slipped into one of disappointment.

"Ah fu-"

Three spears splintered the slates and wood of the roof. One slammed through Sol's skull, two pinned him in the chest. They whipped back. Sol disappeared, leaving behind just and after-image of his shredded body and a mist of blood.

The boy and I watched and made not a single noise.

For hours the pod circled our building, warbling their delight at their catch and booming, hoping for more, but the boy and I were still. As morning turned to afternoon they seemed to move away, though every now and then the one would suddenly unleash a boom right below us. The aching desire to move became a lightning pain and then constant agony, but we sat motionless and silent.

Evening came and the village went quiet, yet still we didn't move. Only when night finally came and the moon was high and clear and frost stung the air did I allow myself to shift. They don't like the dark and they hate the cold.

The boy smiled, then gasped, then sobbed and collapsed forward.

His trousers were slashed open across his hip and his leg was soaked with blood. One of the spears that killed Sol must have glanced off him.

"I didn't cry!" he said.

I gave him a kiss on the cheek.

"A proper little soldier."

NATALIE
Gareth L Powell

Ed stops at a lonely roadside café on a hot autumn night. He drums his fingers on the counter.

"Hey, how about a coffee?" he says. It's late and he's the only customer. The waitress comes over. She's eighteen or nineteen, with long hair and black eyeliner.

"I'm waiting for the water to heat up," she says. She's got a black t-shirt and there's a biro behind her right ear. She looks over Ed's shoulder. "Is that your car?"

He turns in his seat. He's left the Dodge across two handicapped spaces in the empty car park. "Isn't it a beauty?" he says.

She looks at the sweeping tailfins and scratches her chin. There's dried egg on her sleeve. "It looks old" she says. "Is it American?"

Ed nods. He's just borrowed it for the weekend. "I'm on my way up to Hereford, to see the crash site."

She looks him up and down. "Are you a reporter?"

Ed shakes his head. "I'm a photographer."

"Up from London?"

"How did you guess?"

She leans her elbows on the counter. "Are you going to take my picture?"

Ed smiles. "That depends. You haven't told me your name yet."

She brushes the dried egg from her sleeve. "My name's Natalie."

They shake hands. "I'm Ed."

The radio at the back of the kitchen's playing an Elvis song. A truck rattles past on the road outside. "I'll get you that coffee," Natalie says. As she pours it, she looks back at him, over her shoulder.

"There's some wreckage at the top of the valley," she says, "I can show it to you, if you like."

Half an hour later they're rolling up the valley in the Dodge. The single-track road smells hot and the stars overhead are hard and sharp. Natalie's finished her shift. Ed's taken his jacket off. He pulls up his sleeve to show her his tattoo.

"I got that in Amsterdam," he says. Natalie wrinkles her nose. Whenever she moves, her jeans squeak on the seat.

"Take the next left," she says.

Ed lets his sleeve drop. He likes her accent. He touches the brake and down-shifts into the turn.

Natalie points through the windscreen. "It's just up here."

Ed pulls off the road. Up ahead, caught in the headlights, is the wreckage she promised him. It's strewn over the gorse and heather, twisted splinters glinting in the moonlight.

He kills the engine. "Does anyone else know about this?"

Natalie shakes her head. "No-one comes up here much."

It's midnight. Ed opens his door and climbs out, camera in hand. He can smell the heather. He walks over to the nearest fragment. The metal's smooth and warm to the touch. With a dry mouth and sweaty palms, he starts snapping, knowing the pictures he's taking will make his reputation.

Back in the car, Natalie lights a cigarette. She puts her feet up on the dashboard and lets her long hair fall over the back of the seat. She knows to the north there are armed helicopters patrolling the main crash site. But here in the valley, the only thing she hears is the click of Ed's camera in the hot night air.

SOFTLY SOFTLY CATCHEE MONKEY

Shaun C Green

An overcast sky concealed stars and aircraft from sight, just as the tall buildings flanking the quiet thoroughfare endeavoured to conceal the night-time clouds. The street was near-empty of life. There was only the gentle rustling of discarded paper and plastic as it was teased by the breeze.

And there was Joseph, who stumbled from lamppost to bench, from bin to shopfront, his erratic journey from landmark to landmark demonstrating just how pissed he was.

"S'n-not my fault," he told his face, reflected in a shoeshop window. He squinted at himself. "I jusht got paid."

He pushed himself away, leaving greasy fingermarks smeared down the windowpane.

"Should've gotta cab," he mumbled to himself, staggering in the direction of the far end of the street, reasonably confident that it wasn't the way he'd come. "Not chips."

He looked down at his feet, focusing on arranging them so that one trainer was in front of the other, and then the one at the back moved forwards, like so, and then repeat, and - correct the trip with a sideways hop - back into the rhythm, step, step, step-

He realised that there were footsteps behind him, and stopped abruptly. So did the second set of footsteps. Blearily, Joseph glanced around the street in front of him. Nothing, no one. He looked back over his shoulder and couldn't see anyone there either.

He started walking again, and the sound of two sets of footsteps resumed. This time he turned around quickly and caught sight of someone ducking into cover back down the thoroughfare.

"You're not fuckin' funny!" Joseph shouted. He fished a half-eaten bundle of chips out of his pocket, hurling it in the direction of his hiding stalker. This provoked no response.

"Jokers," he grunted to himself. He remained where he stood for several minutes, swaying and glaring, but when no one showed themselves he turned around and began to walk away. The footsteps began again immediately.

This time Joseph whirled around, adrenaline suppressing his drunkenness, and he began to run in a loping, disorganised gait towards his pursuer. He still couldn't make out the figure clearly, but it had a hood up over its head and bright white trainers.

"Fuckin' chav wanker!" Joseph roared. "Fuckin' come on then!"

The figure ducked away to the side again, disappearing into an alleyway that led to another shopping arcade. Joseph headed for the narrow gap in the brick-work, slowing his rush by bouncing off the wall with a gasp. Ahead of him he saw the retreating back of his pursuer, still blurred and indistinct. In his anger he didn't consider the strangeness of the figure being hard to see, when everything around it had become relatively clear in his adrenal rush.

He resumed pursuit, shouting more obscenities at the fleeing figure as it disappeared around a corner. He again skidded to a halt by slamming into the wall and turned his gaze in the direction of the pursued. The figure, still with its hood up, its white trainers now almost searingly bright, the exact features of its clothing still imperceptible, was facing him just a few feet away.

There was a scuffling noise from the entrance to the alley. Joseph glanced to his left and saw another couple of similar-looking figures walking towards him. He turned his attention back to his stalker, saw a fourth silhouette approaching behind it. He opened his mouth to issue a threat, perhaps a plea, but his stalker moved a hand and Joseph collapsed to the ground without resistance. His limbs felt numb, but he could feel the cold and damp pavement against his cheek. He gurgled, trying to speak, and felt saliva run over his lips.

"Monkeys," he heard the first figure say, the English marred by an accent he couldn't recognise. "They're all too easy, no sport at all. Okay, P___, take it up."

Joseph blinked at the still-hazy figure as everything became bathed in blue. He felt his body lift off the ground, and his gorge began to rise.

Joseph's last vision of planet Earth was punctuated by a stream of his own vomit, streaking back down to the pavement below.

ABDUCTION

Dan Pawley

He's on his way home through the last hours of a winter night, orange street-lights smearing and blurring in the misty drizzle, halogen jewels shining back off the wet black road. A few hundred yards further along, and the mist starts to come down fast. Rob's world is shrinking as he walks along, hood up and hands buried in pockets, hiding as much of himself from the night as he can. More mist, and now he can't see the cars before he hears them, a throaty roar drowning out the music in his headphones before the lights are suddenly on him and just as suddenly gone, red tail-lights fading into the ghost world. He turns the music up and keeps walking, head down to keep the wet off his face. The infrequent lights rush by, paying him no heed. And then one set, maybe a little greener-hued than the rest, shoots past him and abruptly halts. A night time prowling cat sees them, hisses and quickly hides behind a nearby bin. The lights rotate in a way no car headlight has ever done, and they start heading slowly and quietly back towards Rob, who is still walking on with his head down and his back turned. They begin to ascend, rising further off the ground as the distance to their target shrinks. By the time they catch up to the oblivious Rob they are several feet above his head.

So fast they seem to have gone from *there* to *there* without travelling the space between, they drop down to pavement level, right where Rob is caught in mid stride. They pause for just a few seconds and then shoot straight up into the sky, quickly lost from view in the mist. The cat comes out of hiding, pads over to where Rob had been stood, sniffs the empty patch of pavement and continues on its way.

ALIEN ABDUCTION
Paul Graham Raven

He lays on the cold hard table, shivering slightly but otherwise motionless. Despite the paralysing drugs, they have restrained his limbs tightly. The stark white light floods down from directly above him; the drugs prevent him from closing his eyes, and the blocks to either side of his head prevent him from turning away for a moment's respite from the glare.

His eyes burn, and he can hardly see at all. In the chilly lucidity of his mind, unaffected by the chemical restraint that keeps his body immobile, he decides that not being able to see is probably a good thing. It means he can't see the incisions they've already inflicted on him.

The clank of heavy feet on metal flooring alerts him to their return – he had hoped, vainly, that perhaps they had done all the tests and experiments they required. But it appears there is more horror to come, further indignities to be visited on him as if he were some lesser lifeform, an experimental animal in a laboratory cage – which to them, he realises, is exactly what he is.

As the chilly metal of some unseen lubricated instrument slips into an orifice which he is unaccustomed to feeling things slid into, he mentally flinches with shock, and fights down a wave of unreasoning fear and unjustified self-loathing. Not for the first time, he wishes he'd never stepped out of the saucer to take a look at those buildings in the first place.

LOST TOYS
Gareth L Powell

When they dropped out of hyperspace, they weren't where they expected to be.

"That's Earth," said Diego.

Beside him, Carla frowned. They were wildly off course. "How did we get here?" she said.

They were lying on couches, jacked into the ship's sensors. The planet turned beneath them, blue and delicate.

"Something must have happened …"

There were sparks against the planet's night side. And when she looked up, there were sparks all over the sky.

"What the hell …?"

She expanded her view. The sparks were ships, thousands of them. Some were maneuvering, others drifting. And in between them, there were other objects - buildings torn loose from their foundations, train carriages, sections of highway …

"Comm traffic's off the scale," Diego said. "Everyone's shouting at once. They're all as confused as we are."

Carla didn't reply. She'd focussed on one of the nearer objects – a tower block tumbling slowly through the vacuum, trailing pipes and cables and loose bricks.

And then she saw something that made her reach for her silver crucifix necklace – a small spacecraft with long instrument booms and a large high-gain antenna. "My God," she said, "it's one of the Voyager probes."

Beside her, Diego swore in Spanish, and crossed himself. "Look, Carla," he said.

He highlighted a tower spinning in the void a few hundred kilometres behind them. As soon as Carla saw it, she recognised it for what it was – the spire of the Church of the Blessed Virgin, from her hometown in Hardfall City, a hundred light years away.

"It's not just us," Diego said with a nervous laugh. "It's everywhere we've been, and everything we've built…" He pulled up an image of the Voyager probe, thrust it at her. "Everything we've ever sent out into space is being returned!"

He pulled off the sensor headset and sat up on his couch. Feeling him move, Carla squeezed her crucifix.

"What are you saying?"

Diego rubbed his face. When he looked at her, she could see the whites of his eyes.

"We're being tidied up," he said.

THE EMPEROR'S NEW FORCE FIELD

Gareth D Jones

The Emperor's fleet swept through the Galaxy, conquering world after world. Not a shot was fired by his mighty ships. Everyone knew that fighting was pointless. The Emperor's new force field was invincible; nothing could harm his vessels.

When dozens of the Emperor's battle ships arrived in the Glasburg system, the local fleet commander prepared his immediate surrender. Their own ships, modern and fearsome as they were, stood no chance.

Archibald McNeil, asteroid prospector, was none to pleased that his livelihood was about to be ruined. In a futile gesture of defiance he fired his mining laser at the nearest of the invading ships. There was a brief flash of energy impact followed by a puff of debris ejected from the hull.

"Drat," said the Emperor's new Admiral, as the secret of their invincible shield was exposed and his fleet was destroyed around him.

GREAT OLD ONE EX MACHINA

Dan Pawley

In the late summer of 20--, strange events began to affect the globe's commu-
nication networks. Large numbers of people, many of them respected members
of their societies, claimed to have heard bizarre noises during telephone calls.
Conversations were being drowned out by bubbling and rushing sounds, as if
the caller were underwater. Engineers sent to inspect the affected systems could
offer no solution. These occurrences lasted a week or so, and drew amused com-
ments from the newspapers before being forgotten in the normal course of
events.

A short while later, online computer forums and blogs began to comment
on a strange new virus. Once a machine was infected, an unusual icon would
appear in the system tray. It seemed to represent a humanoid character, but one
with wings, and what was agreed, after much inspection of the tiny pixellated
image, to be a set of tentacles around its face. The virus spread quickly, but as
the icon seemed to be connected to no program and the virus had no negative
effect in its host computer, attention moved on once again.

One Professor Ward of Miskatonic University, however, did not forget
these events. He advanced a theory that these strange happenings were linked,
and furthermore that they had had their genesis in a maritime accident some
months previously. The cable laying ship *Maria Elena* had been working in the
Pacific when it was lost with all hands. Professor Ward had procured a record-
ing of the last transmission from the stricken vessel, on which the captain could
be heard shouting nonsense about the sea boiling and buildings emerging from
the waves. The owners of the *Maria Elena* admitted that the captain had had a
drink problem, and that he had probably been suffering hallucinations which

caused him to lose control of his ship, with tragic consequences.

Professor Ward, on the other hand, believed that the unfortunate craft had encountered a legendary submerged city known as R'lyeh, which was home to a monstrous creature called Cthulhu, one of what he called The Great Old Ones. These, he averred, were impossibly ancient and malevolent creatures from beyond space and time. Thanks to the sinking of the *Maria Elena*, they had gained access to mankind's undersea cables and fibre optic networks. These creatures could control thought, he warned. Was it so hard to suppose they could also infiltrate our telephony systems? He feared that Cthulhu was planning a dreadful re-emergence, and that the noises on the telephone lines and the mysterious icon had been his first fumbling attempts to influence our technology. Naturally, the professor and his claims were soundly ridiculed.

Then came Black Tuesday, when every computer connected to the internet failed simultaneously. Home firewalls and business security systems crumbled, leaving blank screens worldwide. An hour after the initial failure, while helpdesks were still reeling, the computers spontaneously reactivated. They were exactly as before, save for a string of words in an unintelligible language sat across the centre of their screens:

Ph'nglui mglw'nafh Cthulhu R'lyeh wgah'nagl fhtagn

The appearance of two key words from his theory immediately focused attention back on Professor Ward. Yet the professor could offer no further advice. Shortly after the message appeared Ward had hung himself, his body discovered twisting in the glow of the tell-tale letters on his screen. He left no note, save for what was taken to be a translation of the alien words :

In his house at R'lyeh dead Cthulhu waits dreaming

That was six weeks ago. Operators have been able to use their computers as normal since Black Tuesday, although the message has proved impossible to remove. Four weeks ago, two bizarre glyphs appeared on every screen under the original text. The right hand glyph changed daily and the left hand one every three days, leading some to speculate that it is a countdown of sorts, although no one has been prepared to guess what it may be counting down to.

Yesterday the left glyph disappeared. This was widely interpreted to mean that the countdown had entered single figures and was now into its final three days. Today the radio has reported a massive undersea eruption, very near the spot where the Maria Elena was lost. Seismological equipment indicates that a large section of sea bed in the area is rising towards the ocean surface.

I do not know what will happen tomorrow.

FORTUNE COOKIE
Justin Pickard

To Noah, the Chinese restaurant channelled clips from a hundred badly dubbed kung-fu movies. There was the tank of exotic fish into which the katana-wielding goons would be thrown; here was the frosted plate glass through which the elderly kingpin would be thrown, plummeting to his death; and there was the door with the 'no entry' sign which would inevitably lead to the ill-lit underground headquarters from which the family coordinated their money laundering / prostitution / drug smuggling activities. He tried explaining this to his date, but she seemed less than entirely convinced.

Clearing her throat, she explained how it was more likely that the fish tank was made from shatter-proof plastic, and how it would be impossible for anyone – even an elderly, moustachioed master criminal – to die from injuries sustained in a fall from the ground floor. She was smiling, though. So perhaps, on some level, she understood what he meant?

He told her about the full extent of his Wuxia collection. She told him about her job in publishing. He explained how it was cheaper for him to live in his parents basement, which was actually quite spacious now that he'd moved the boxes. She smiled encouragingly.

But his suspicions about her were properly confirmed when, in a lull in the conversation, she gestured for him to lean in. Glancing sideways at the waitress, who hovered in the background like some kind of vulture, Noah's date closed her hand on his. She believed him. And If Noah was willing to distract the girl, she'd go and investigate the underground headquarters, allowing him to follow later. Say, in half an hour. Heart thumping, Noah nodded. He ordered another glass of lemonade, and a couple of fortune cookies. The waitress disappeared into the kitchen, and Noah's date made a beeline for the door. Glancing back over her shoulder, she winked, and the door swung shut behind her.

The fortune cookies came, along with the drink, but Noah's date was nowhere to be seen. What if she'd been captured? After twenty-two minutes, he could bear it no longer. While the waitress was engaged in argument with a heavy-set gentleman on a table in the far corner, Noah stood up slowly, sidled over the door, took a deep breath, and leapt into the cleaning cupboard.

There was a mop, a bucket, and several bottles of cleaning fluid. The window was open, and someone had stacked a couple of boxes against the wall. Noah sighed, explained to the irate waitress that he'd simply been looking for the toilet, and returned to his table.

So much for the criminal gang. Heck, so much for his date. Momentarily losing himself in the pattern of gas bubbles rising in his glass of lemonade, Noah broke into the larger of the fortune cookies. Now, that was odd - instead of a piece of paper, there was a small ziploc bag, which seemed to contain some kind of ... white ... powder.

Shit, thought Noah, as he met the less-than-friendly gaze of the guy at the other table, *Not again.*

CLICHÉ

Neil Beynon

"I don't want it," said the woman, handing the box back to the man. He looked crestfallen taking the intricately carved cube in his large ponderous hands. The woman smiled gently at him as you would a child who had just learnt their first unpleasant truth about the world.

"It would never work," she explained. "I'm just not like that."

"But I meant it," he said. "It's meant to be you."

"No," she said. "It's not. You're young, you'll learn. Life is not that clichéd."

She turned and walked away from him, her stiletto heels clipping on the concrete pavement as she did. He flipped over the lid, gazed on the contents with watery blue eyes.

"I meant it," he said quietly, then louder. "I meant it."

She turned back briefly, she did not smile and after a brief glance she was walking again. He closed the box that held his heart and locked it before dropping it into his bag.

THAI CURRY
Gareth L Powell

After dinner, we bought a bottle of wine and took a taxi back to her flat. The fire escape opened onto a flat section of roof, still warm from the day's heat.

"Sit down, make yourself comfortable," Nina said.

She smelled of patchouli. She wore a black cocktail dress and had her hair chopped into a platinum Warhol mop. There was a silver pendant around her neck and – when she finally took the dress off – a vertical scar between her breasts.

She saw me looking at it and touched it with her fingers. It made her uncomfortable.

"I once lost my heart," she explained.

THE DECISION THAT CHANGED THE LIFE OF FABRICE COLLISEO

Martin McGrath

A life does not flow evenly from spring to the ocean, its passage is broken by rapids and falls, twists and turns. The choices we make define a life's course and some decisions take us over a threshold where the effort necessary to backtrack, to paddle against the turbulence and cross to another stream, requires more strength and dedication than most can muster.

Which decisions will plunge us over a precipice? We may not consciously take a decision at all, but drift into the maw of the momentous. But, even when conscious of the act of choosing, sometimes the greatest consequences spring from the apparently inconsequential. Some lives change by turning right instead of left, leaving rather than staying, or saying "I love you" but meaning "I want you."

But a few people know, the very moment they make their choice, that their life has changed forever.

For Fabrice Colliseo that moment came early. He was barely out of his teens when he made up his mind to kill a man. That man was Alfonso, clever, handsome and beloved Alfonso. Alfonso the priest. Alfonso, his brother.

Fabrice did not have his brother's fancy education, but knew enough of theology to know that, having made his choice, he was as guilty of the sin as if he'd already dipped his hands in his brother's blood. The actual committing of the murder was inconsequential and could wait for the perfect moment. But the knowledge that he now bore a mark that could not be confessed and could never be forgiven resigned Fabrice to his damnation.

And so Fabrice was set free.

Fabrice had been a shy boy whose fear had turned sour in his belly and made the man withdrawn and untrusting. He had been morose when sober but bellicose in wine.

Now, reborn, Fabrice had nothing to fear since nothing could be worse than damnation. So Fabrice relaxed. He joked with neighbours, his laughter echoed around the high-walled streets of his home town, he offered a helping hand to all in need, he devoted time and money to good works and soon he became the most welcome visitor in any house in the town.

Though hardly handsome Fabrice was well set financially and his new demeanour and the high regard with which the people of the town came to hold him made him attractive. Soon he found himself with a pretty wife who was devoted to her husband. Their first child came quickly, and many more followed.

"What was it that brought so great a change in you?" Fabrice's mother asked, with the boldness of the aged. It was a Sunday when all the family had gathered together and Alfonso had finished offering Grace.

"My brother," Fabrice replied without hesitation.

"Of course," she said. "Alfonso."

The answer made Fabrice's mother happy for it confirmed that everything that was good in her life flowed from her saintly, priested son. But Fabrice watched the way Alfonso bowed his head in mock humility and remade his vow to strike down his brother.

Years went by.

The mother of Fabrice and Alfonso died. She was ancient but still her loss was sudden. Fabrice held her hand as she faded away but her last words were for her Alfonso, then far away tending to some bishop.

Fabrice's upward trajectory continued. His decency and honesty saw his reputation grow and he enjoyed both material comfort and the respect of almost all those who knew him. He was a man of standing now, not just in his own commune but in the whole department. Even lords from Paris were known to descend upon him for his advice when dealing with local affairs.

The fortunes of Alfonso did not quite wane, but his assured ascent did falter. Without the belief and the constant driving force of his mother he seemed to loose momentum. His rise within the clergy reached what his mother would have regarded as a rather paltry peak with his appointment as parish priest. His belly widened and his youthful beauty faded, his hair thinned and his skin became blotched in a way that suggested he was becoming too fond of wine.

Then came the scandal.

A girl, a maid in the parish house, ran through the streets weeping with her dress torn. Her father came to Fabrice. He was sorry to involve a good man in this, he said, but the town knew that his daughter was not the first to have born such indignity. Something must be done.

The bishop became involved and Alfonso was cast into that internal exile which the Catholic Church has had so long to perfect. There was to be no public humiliation, for that would damage the church. Alfonso was "ill" and that sickness would prevent him continuing with his duties as parish priest and Fabrice took it upon himself to generously compensate the maid's family. The people of the town came together to celebrate Alfonso's years of service and even those few angry enough to express their feelings in public bit their tongues out of respect for Fabrice.

But Alfonso knew that he was disgraced.

Fabrice offered Alfonso refuge in his own house. He moved the old priest into a room high in the eaves and fed him and provided all the wine the old man could drink. Alfonso brooded and spoke only to his brother. Fabrice became his brother's keeper, his confidante and even his confessor. Alfonso was worn out, his mind was often confused and the disappointments of his life stacked up behind rheumy eyes to force out floods of tears at unpredictable moments. Before long his health failed and Alfonso refused to leave his bed.

Now, at last, it was time.

Fabrice climbed the stone stairs from the kitchens through his family's rooms and the servants' quarters. He carried a bowl of soup, a bottle of red wine and bread – his brother's lunch. Alfonso's room was higher still, up rough wooden steps. He pushed up open the door into the dim room, slivers of the afternoon light sliced the room capturing for a moment, swirling galaxies of dust.

Alfonso was asleep. Fabrice laid the bowl, bottle and bread on a small table and approached the bed.

He looked down on his brother and it occurred to him that he no longer had to do this. He had surpassed the priest. Looking down on the old man before him he felt only pity.

And yet he had made this choice long ago. The river had flowed this way for too long, its path was too deeply eroded for it now to leap its banks and start of a new course. The choice he had made had brought him happiness, strength and pride. This was the price that had to be paid.

He pulled a pillow from beneath Alfonso's head.

The priest woke, smacking his lips, blinking and staring at his brother.

"Is it time?"

"Yes," said Fabrice and lowered the pillow. "It is time."

THE ALLITERATI
Gareth D Jones

"Greetings, Gaius," said the dark robed man as he stepped bare foot down the icy stone corridor. A shorter, balding man in matching black robe nodded at him from the doorway to his small cell.

"Salutations, Silas," he said, and fell in behind, joining a steady stream of berobed men as they emerged from the low dormitory building. The smaller and weaker of the planet's two suns had just topped the horizon and was shining blearily through the clouds that swaddled the sky. The yard was chill and damp from the night's rain.

"Wet weather's worsening," Silas commented.

"'Tis true," Gaius agreed. There was not much other conversation as the monks crossed to the simple stone chapel that had been the heart of their order for over a century. More, certainly, than the silent orders that had taken root on some planets; but here there was certainly more time spent constructing sentences than uttering them. They often fell back on the same well worn phrases to communicate the necessities of the day.

Twenty or thirty men entered the chapel and stood by their pews. The abbot stood before them and raised his hands in a gesture of benevolence.

"Stay standing silently," he intoned. After a moment's contemplation he lowered his hands. "Sit, search souls, surrender sin." The mostly silent service continued for long minutes. Afterwards they emerged into the yard where both suns were now attempting to banish the early morning gloom.

"Today's tasks?" Silas asked his friend. Gaius thought for a moment.

"Gathering garden groceries," he smiled. "Gladly."

Silas smiled in return and went about his own chore of gathering quail eggs. He could think of no alliteration for it.

TEST DRIVE
Justin Pickard

Liquid mildew, chemical pine and cigarette butts. Lilting accents strained through radio static. The dim lights of an industrial leviathan – heavy with freight – navigating the channel. The rustling foil of a crisp packet, followed by Tom's enthusiastic crunching.

Her face up against the glass, Sam squints through the grime and muck, and out into the murk. Her right leg, in a moment of treachery, surrenders to the numbness. Still, he had assured her that this evening would be worth seeing – the first gasp of something that could change everything.

When pressed, he had done his best to explain and she, in turn, had tried her best to understand. But it hadn't quite stuck.

"I'm sorry, H, but I lost you at the bit with the strings." Sam bites her bottom lip and, squirming in her seat, inadvertently elbows Dylan in the ribs. He yelps. The glove compartment snaps shut.

"Look, just forget I said anything about the damned strings."

"But-"

"Believe me, it's not going to make the slightest bit of difference." He catches her expression in the rear view mirror, and cranes his neck round to face her. "I mean, I've got two, almost three, years of this under my belt, and even I'm not entirely sure why it works."

"Right." says Dylan, "But you're sure that it's safe?"

"Totally."

To Sam, Hywel's response sounds too confident, too polished. She hesitates, but doesn't say anything. Turning the question over in her mind, examining it from all angles, she searches for a gut instinct that is, for once, conspicuous in its absence. Nothing there. No answers.

"Reckon that's Zoe?" asks Dylan, gesturing at a light just beyond the hedge-row.

"Must be." says Tom, entrenching himself in the sagging upholstery of the main passenger seat. "She said she'd be out, oh-" He glances at his watch. "At least twenty minutes ago. Probably more."

As the light approaches, Hywel winds down the window.

"About bloody time. We'd almost given up on you."

Close cropped hair - recently bleached "as a symbol of, like, autonomy" - and wide staring eyes, Zoe twists her torch, plunging them back into twilight. Blanking Hywel, she pokes her head through the other window. Automatically, Sam smiles. Zoe is nice. Safe. Inoffensive.

"'Sup, Sam? Dylan. There enough room for me in the front, Tom?"

Hywel glances over at Tom, who sighs, then nods. Zoe grins.

"Ace."

Somehow, Tom disentangles himself from Hywel's overenthusiastic exercise in wiring, and clambers into the back. Dumping her canvas shoulder-bag some-where in the vehicle's murky depths, Zoe perches on the passenger seat. As she leans over to fiddle with the radio, Hywel bats her hand away from the dials.

"Don't" he says, firmly, "It'll interfere with the electronics."

While Tom struggles to accommodate the mysterious contents of a large, black bin-liner, Zoe turns to the others, rolling her eyes in mock exasperation.

"Did you sort out the interface?" asks Hywel, kick-starting the ignition.

"Yeah." Tom reaches into the black sack. "I borrowed the departmental lap-top. It's got ten hours of battery." With a theatrical flourish, he reveals the white monster, triumphantly holding it aloft.

"Simple as that?" asks Zoe, clearly impressed.

"Well, there were forms." Tom's eyes glaze over. "But, on the plus side, we've until Monday." He flips open its lid, and taps at the buttons. It beeps.

"Awesome." Zoe beams.

Sam yelps, the centre of gravity shifting under her as Hywel takes a sharp right at the crossroads.

"Believe me, Sam," he says, stifling a chuckle, "There's worse than that to come." Slowing to fiddle with the clutch, he turns to Tom. "Are we ready?"

Tom is still struggling with a box of floppy disks.

"Hang on, dude." He selects one, seemingly at random, and tentatively pokes it into the appropriate drive. There's a click, and Tom nods, satisfied. "Ready when you are."

"Right. Hang on, guys."

Hywel yanks the clutch and pushes his foot to the floor, while Tom bashes away frantically on the Mac's keyboard. There is a loud beep, and the landscape drops away – replaced by a textured blackness. Lurching sideways, Hywel's ears pop, Zoe sneezes, and Sam's fighting back acidic bile. Unsuccessfully, as it turns out.

"Woah." says Dylan, ignoring the guttural retching. "Like, where are we?"

"Don't suppose anyone has tissues?" asks Sam, quietly. Silence.

"What happens next?" asks Zoe, her palms pressed against the passenger window.

"I'm not entirely sure," admits Hywel, reluctantly passing Sam a well-used tissue, "I mean, we programmed the coordinates for Bangor, but-"

"Bangor?" asks Sam, clearly confused. "That's, like, a hundred miles -"

"Shit." Tom's voice is carefully calculated, devoid of emotion. Another beep.

"What? What's happened?"

"The box just died."

The silence races outwards, subsuming everything in its path. They sit in the darkness for an eternity – five victims of entropy, individually contemplating their fate.

Well, almost.

"Custard cream, anyone?"

More silence. Eyebrows heavy, Hywel and Sam exchange looks. Dylan clears his throat.

"Yeah," he says, eventually, "Go on then."

LIFE IS A WHEEL
Neil Beynon

Life is a wheel. It turns on a spoke and runs along the asphalt taking you to new places all the while spinning on the same bearings.

I love to cycle, the wind on my back, the pure rhythm of the pedals a mantra that calms the mind and cleanses the soul. I feel better already.

It's funny, now I'm rolling down the hill I can't even remember what we were arguing about, stupid. I can see her now, before the argument, the tawny sunlight on her smooth thigh thrown casually over the duvet. As she wakes the beams catching the red flecks in her hair; the hidden fire in her brown locks, the pink bloom on her cheek where her head rested on the pillow: I am so damn lucky.

I'm going to call her as soon as I get into the office, tell her I'm sorry, and maybe buy her some, shi--

Life is a wheel. It turns on a spoke and runs along the asphalt taking you to new places all the while spinning on the same bearings.

I love to cycle ...

STURGEON'S LAW

Paul Graham Raven

James stopped scraping and put his trowel down in the muck.

"Who was Sturgeon, anyway?"

"Dunno," piped Alex, still elbow-deep in the Heap. "Never wiki'd it; we can take a look when we get back down-town and into the cloud."

Two weeks outside corporate Britain, and James still hadn't adjusted to not being online wherever he went. Alex had told him that once he had some local credit, he could pay a monkey to revalidate his ID on the satellites. But for now, while he tried to build enough credit to get himself settled and independent, he had to make do with the municipal net down-town.

Outside of town – out here on the Heap - he had to make do with Alex, who knew a lot of practical stuff about staying afloat in New Southsea. Getting that information was tricky, though; the kid's mind darted like an evening mosquito.

"So," said James, "what's this law, then?"

Alex looked up at James, flicked something small at him, and grinned. "Ninety percent of everything is crap!"

James picked up the bit and brushed the mud from it. "This Sturgeon was a scavver as well, then?" he asked.

"Nah, not a scavver. I think he was from before we needed scavving. Or maybe not before we needed it, but before we were forced into it, get me?"

"Sure," lied James.

"Anyway, don't matter who he was – he's just some guy the Old Booker goes on about when he's teaching me to read," said Alex. "Waves around at all them piles of old books he's got, shouts about Sturgeon's Law. Usually after he's been up to the stills on his roof. He's funny, those times; not like some drinkers."

James looked down at the thing Alex had thrown at him; a muddied slice of aluminium no bigger than his thumbnail, with holes and grooves cut and folded into it.

"So what have old books got do with scavving, then?"

"Well, this is my theory, not the Old Booker's," said Alex, still digging. "But I borrowed it from him, and he got it from this Sturgeon guy. See, the Booker says ninety percent of all books are crap. But here's the thing – two different people will pick a different ten percent as the good stuff. See?"

"Still lost, kid."

"Ah, it's easy. Look – scav is like the books. One guy looks, sees ninety per-cent crap, takes the good ten, yeah? But another guy looks, and he sees his ten percent in the ninety the other guy left behind."

"So you're trying to say that everything out here is almost worthless, but almost all of it is worth something to somebody?"

"Bang on, professor! Like that in your hand; TwenCen ringpulls, from drink containers. Tiny, hard to find – but pure ally. And I know a guy who'll pay three credits per hundred, 'cause they're just the right size and shape for some engine part he makes for the boaters."

Three credits was enough to keep a man afloat for half a week, James knew. Not living the high life, but well clear of starvation and charity. "So I need to look out for these ringpulls, then? Is that it?"

The kid sat back for a moment. "Nah, you're not seeing it yet – you gotta look out for *everything*, especially at first. That's the thing – if you wanna work the Heap, you don't need to *learn* the Heap, beyond knowing which bits'll kill you and which won't."

He leaned back over his little pit and started scraping again. "You gotta learn the market back in town, man. That's why we don't work too late out here, see? Gotta get back in time for some biz."

James stared at Alex: a grubby teenager with a false leg digging through a hill of compacted waste, who supported himself and his mother by unearthing junk and selling it on. A far cry from the cannibal anarchists James had seen on the arcology newsfeeds.

"Come on, man, dig!" called Alex. "Find one ringpull, maybe find lots more in the same area. I can't give you everything I find; me mum would kill me."

James picked up his borrowed trowel, and started scraping.

GREY MATTER
Shaun C Green

I see him walking by me, snobby longnose, digits rubbin' 'n tappin' at temple, every day, see, I see. Every day on his way from metro to tower, tower to metro, few hundred feet, rubbing 'n tabbing. Hides his eyes behind dark glasses. See a lot of dark glasses these days. Richer types, bluer blood 'n such as I, got little micro-chipses in the head. Some tells me they thinks faster, 'members more, even things as never happen.

Makes me think, this. If'n they can 'member things as never happen, they can forget things as did. Colour me fair jealous a' that.

So I starts watchin' him closer-like, this head-scratcher, scalp-poker, itchy-itchy at the little wires and plastics under the skin and hair and bone. Sev'ral times in a month I see him trip, hand leaves head, fingers fan out, he catches his balance. Roun' him there's kids, poorer folk, shopworkers 'n tourists with snappy-cams, they's snigger at him, moment o' derision for the richies that sit up top an' shit on 'em all. Then he's off agin and they's just a crowd once more, sullen-like that they gets no 'puter brains to get 'em on top an' keep 'em there.

Still, little enjoy-your-trips make me thinks, see, not needin' no extra wirin'. Fella don't notice stuff as bein' about him when he head-scratchin' like that, too busy wit' his numbers and facts and jugglin' little en-sic-lo-peeds in the grey 'n green matter, like. Sorta distraction a cunnin' type could take advantage of. Mayhap a cunnin' type such as I.

Little problem, mind. Everyone watch him when he trip. Everyone watch him, all the time. Lil' side-eyes shootin' resentment, waitin' for the stumble-tumble, watchin' and waitin' for the mighty to fall. Mmm.

So's I leave my cubby-hole, little place-o-safety, every man's home a fortress. Creep along through the darks that flank the light and bright streets. Watchin' ol' longnose, rubbin' an' tappin' an' countin'.

Don't take long for old man opportunity to come a knockin'. Turns out to be at a cubby door in the metro pisser. Big man gotta weak bladder, dodgy bowel, too much caviar in the lunchbox, somethin' like. But in he goes and after I creeps and door he shuts behind, lockin' me out, big room aroun' the small, another man shakin' hisself out agin the piss-tray.

Time to use the ol' noggin. I finds a cubby next to my scalp-poker, lock the door behind me natural-soundin'. Wait wait wait, tick tock tick tock of a watch next door. I hear the other fella outside up an' leave, not waitin' to wash his hands. I tries not to titter: rough-sleepers got better hygiene than some housed fellas.

But I don't let rip, no no, it's time to be quiet-like. First up, peek under the stall-wall. Black shoes. Leather. Expensive. Socks, trousers, belt, all rucked down.

Next it's up--careful, quiet now--and peek over the stall-wall. I see him, finger-tappin' away, still hidin' his eyes, still in his own little world. Perfect. With a slither-slither and a scufflin', I haul myself up and over quick and sharp-like. And before he catches up with himself I've got a hand over his mouth and his glasses are hangin' off and at last I see his eyes. They're full o' fear. All his numbers gone run away.

Then I thinks: alla this time, I bin after this guy 'cuz of what's bein' in his head. Ain't been usin' what's in mine. How's I expectin' to get them chippy brains outta there?

His chin's all smooth unner my hand. Smooth like a babby or a bottle. I stare at him, he stare at me, an' there's not a twitch from us. S'a *Meh-hee-can* standoff, *compadre*, I can't move unless you do! So I thinks, an' thinks a bit more, an' then I gets it. I smile big teeth at poor scared little man and reach out to him, out to his headfaceeyes ...

An' then, quick as a lightnin'-flash, I'm outta the cubby, big man made little behind me, confused an' starin' at the real. I've a skip anna hop anna trip anna skip, wearin' my new dark glasses, a-rubbing 'n tapping at temple, with bigbig thoughts in the ol' grey matter.

THE RED KING'S NURSERY
Gareth L Powell

When the ship located him, the man was sitting in an elegant drawing room on the southern wing of the Winter Palace. The desk before him was littered with annotated maps and reports and he was methodically loading a crude but deadly-looking revolver. Sounds of fighting drifted up from the city below, muffled slightly by the blizzard.

The ship watched him for a moment through the snow piling against the balcony windows, and then projected a remote unit into the room. The man looked up at it floating beneath the chandelier with no obvious surprise. The remote unit shook melting snowflakes from its triangular casing and settled slowly onto the broad mantelpiece.

"Good evening, Lawrence. How goes your little revolution?"

The man finished loading the revolver and pushed the barrel into the top of his fur-lined boot.

"I have nothing to say to you."

An explosion near the palace gates shook the chandelier, jangling its glass beads. Shouts came from the courtyard as the guards took up defensive positions along the outer wall. Lawrence rose and walked toward the door.

"It's nearly time," the remote said from its perch.

"Not interested." The man extracted a cutlass from the umbrella stand and ran an experimental thumb along the blade. He seemed satisfied with the sharpness and carefully pushed it through his belt. Machine gun fire clattered somewhere nearby.

"What do you mean you're not interested?" The remote rose into the air. "It's your turn."

The lights dimmed as further explosions rattled the glass in the windows.

Lawrence pulled an enormous and filthy greatcoat from the hat stand and slipped it around his shoulders.

"I'm happy enough here," he said.

The remote floated toward him. "How can you be happy here?" it asked. "You're hopelessly outnumbered, outgunned and surrounded."

"I'll do better next time."

"Rubbish."

A biplane clattered overhead in the darkness. The remote moved forward until it was only centimetres from the man's face.

"It's your turn," it said. "You have absolutely no hope of survival here. The game is over. It's time to grow up."

As if to illustrate the point, bullets shattered the window, spraying flying splinters of glass and wood into the room. Lawrence crouched on one knee behind the table and drew his revolver.

"We should be going," the remote said.

Outside, the snow stopped falling and the noise of the approaching battle faded. The grandfather clock by the fireplace stopped ticking.

Lawrence stood up. "Hey, I wasn't finished."

He threw his revolver onto the table, let his shoulders slump. "It's not fair," he said.

The remote settled onto the table. "It's time to go," it said. "Your parents are waiting for you, in the hospital."

Lawrence looked up. "My parents?"

"Yes, nice people. You'll like them."

The walls of the room were fading now, breaking apart pixel by pixel.

"Okay," Lawrence said. "What happens now?"

"Just close your eyes and relax. Oh, and Lawrence?"

"Yes?"

"Happy Birthday."

LEAVING THE WORLD
Martin McGrath

Sept sat cross-legged in the centre of an ordinary living room and pulled The World from his head one wire at a time. Blood ran down the pale skin on his back, staining the blue shorts that were the only clothes he wore, and spread across the wheat coloured carpet in a growing pool. The furniture, stylish, modern and tasteful had been pushed into the corners. The screens were off. Pictures and paintings were turned to the wall. A small scattering of provisions and necessary tools surrounded Sept, everything else had been cast aside. He had prepared for this. He was ready.

He ignored the blood on the floor but every few minutes he had to stop to push back the flow of thick crimson that threatened to blind him. He didn't need his eyes, he could finish this without them, but the stinging pain was distracting.

He ran a finger along his scalp until he felt the slight rise of skin that marked where a wire had burrowed through and then he dug his long thumb nail (he'd let it grow specially for this moment) into the flesh sliding it forward until he felt the slight resistance that showed he'd hooked the wire.

He'd winced at first, each time he'd jammed the nail into his own scalp, but by now his head was dull, distant mass of pain and each new wound was barely noticed. The contents of the empty bottle of vodka at his feet had helped.

With his thumbnail under a wire, he'd follow it forward to the point where it met a connector and burrowed its way through his skull. Here Sept paused for a moment, closing his eyes, softly licking his lips, taking a longer breath, holding on to the moment of anticipation. And then he'd flick his thumb forward and there would be the slightest "pop!" as the wire was freed from its connector and a little bit of The World slipped away.

Sept could not let himself get distracted by this small step closer to freedom, for this was a moment of struggle. The wire, part-mechanical, part living thing was programmed to reattach itself and it would writhe with surprising energy. The thing wasn't strong, but it was quick and Sept had to use both hands to shove it into the throbbing bundle that he'd corralled on the back of his neck with an old red rubber band.

And then the process began again. Working with his thumb, methodically from left to right, finding each wire, popping it free, tying it up - and all the while The World slipped away. There were hundreds of wires, it was a slow job.

He paused. Reached for one of the bottles of water that he'd set out before him, took as sip, and then poured half the bottle over his head. He wasn't worried about infection, but the blood on his head was clotting quickly, tangling his hair and forming a thick, crackling coating on his scalp that made finding the wires more difficult. Pink water sloshed across the floor, flowing up to the edge of a white rug and then ebbing, leaving behind pink-stained woollen fibres.

Sept went back to removing The World.

Warning lights were flashing now, even when he closed his eyes. Screeds of system warnings scrolled up across his eyeline. He tried to blink them away, but the interface responses were sluggish. External links were powered down, but he kept having to deny emergency contacts to bring an engineer.

Pop! Pop! Pop!

The visual interface failed.

Sept sighed. The World was almost gone. Lights flickered as the system attempted to reroute. It came up for a second then crashed in a rainbow smear.

Almost done.

Pop! Pop!

He grabbed the thick cord of writhing wires, following them to where they came together on his neck, at the top of his spine. Here The World box sat and whirred at the interface between body and mind.

Sept gave the wires a gentle, experimental tug.

This was the most dangerous moment. The wires from The World threaded throughout the body. If he got this wrong, the stories said, he could expect paralysis or even instant death.

He paused for a moment.

Did he really want this?

Suddenly the effects of the vodka seemed to leave him. All at once he was aware of the steel-sharp pain that ripped at his scalp and the tepid fluids pooled uncomfortably around him and the chill smell of blood.

The World was gone.

He was all alone.

And he wasn't afraid.

Sept gripped the wires that connected his brain to The World and he yanked.

THE NATIVES ARE RESTLESS TONIGHT

Dan Pawley

We were on the hills high above the city. It was a clear night, and a thousand stars shone hard and bright in the sky over our heads, so close I almost believed I could reach up, grab a fistful in my hand and scatter them like diamonds on the ground around my feet. Down in the valley, the city lights were dirtier and shabbier. We looked back on them and knew that after what we had done today they would be just as closed to us as the stars.

We shouldered our packs and walked on, all of us trying to appear undaunted, but I'm convinced the others felt the same churning mixture of fear, wonder and relief in their stomachs that I did. When we heard a roar behind us, we turned back to see a shuttle lifting out of the city, probably carrying troops and officials back to one of the giant craft still in high orbit. I watched it rise on its pillar of fire, thinking that tomorrow those Uyoku would be congratulating themselves on a lucky escape.

There were old farm cottages further up in the hills, tumbledown stone buildings that had survived earlier border invasions by the English, who came first as conquerors and then as tourists and property developers. Owen was confident they would outlast the Uyoku Hegemony as well. We would still be nominally inside the Occupied Territories, but there were enough sympathetic locals to keep us supplied and hidden, and we reckoned the authorities wouldn't be looking for us so close to the scene of the crime. We'd be there in less than an hour, ready to lay low as long as we had to. I wondered idly if we would be close enough to hear the blasts.

FATIMA'S FUNERAL
Justin Pickard

Nights are the worst. At some base level, the shock threw her fight-or-flight reflex, flooding her system with wave after wave of adrenaline. Hours spent staring at the apartment ceiling, Etienne snoring contently beside her. She waits for the wide-eyed exhaustion to retreat. And, when she does finally drop off, the occasional burst of distant gunfire seeps into her subconscious, warping her dreams. Brotherhood sympathisers, chanting in broken French. NDP leaders melting into the glittering blue of pirated photovoltaics. Amidst the hollering and raucous applause, only their inane grimaces linger, outlined in fire against a sky of deep scarlet.

Her mind is still reeling, raw and unanchored. A whole world, snatched from her and hundreds - if not thousands - of others like her. If there had been a warning, they could have prepared. On. Then off. Yanked from the data-streams and thrust, bawling, into the angry reality that she'd spent the last six months trying her hardest to ignore.

Fatima's funeral marks the fourth day since the pulse. Four days without the mesh, and three nights of fragmenting sleep and feverish hallucinations. Sam had never been particularly close to Fatima, but the funeral is bearable enough. The gentle drone of family elders is a welcome respite from the smog of su-perliminal panic. But a couple of hours is all she gets. Despite data blackout, curfews, and gunfire, the various cousins and hangers-on seem all too eager to return home. Politely avoiding Sam's speculations about recent developments, they make their excuses and leave; a cloud of pursed lips and pragmatic eye-brows, picking their way through the City of the Dead.

Home in time for dinner.

In their absence, she sits, staring out over the graves of those long dead. The sun is low, hanging ominously against the dark smoke of the western horizon. But with a good few hours before the curfew, and Etienne watching over the boys, she can afford to take some time for herself. A couple of minutes to Be, without having to Do.

"Are you okay, Samira?" With someone's hand on her shoulder, she freezes. "You look- well, like you haven't slept in weeks." The voice is rich, smooth, and unpleasantly familiar. Of course, she had heard the footsteps, she must have. She just hadn't been listening to them. A subtle difference, but an important one. Warily, she looks up.

"Karim." she says, flatly. "Wasn't expecting to see you here, of all places."

He's taller than she remembers, and his greasy locks are longer. Still, he is wearing the jacket. That grotty, battered leather jacket - by now, as much a part of him as his limbs or head.

"Well, no," he admits, shifting uneasily from foot to foot. "And under normal circumstances, I wouldn't have come, but -"

He glances over his shoulder, leaving the comment to hang, unfinished. To Sam, he looks downright furtive.

"But what?" she asks, prompting him to continue.

"I don't think I've got much time," he says, lowing his voice. "And I need to ask a favour of you. If you're willing, of course."

Karim waits, hopefully. Eventually, she nods.

He lends her his wearable to look at the files, as they pick their way between the tombs. Nanofab plans for seventeen items. A statue of a husband and wife, a bust of some historical figure, a large urn, and a bunch of other, smaller arte-facts. He claims to have acquired them from a former curator at the national museum; a Brotherhood supporter who'd copied the 'prints after the bomb, but before the NDP recaptured Tahrir square.

"After the bomb?" Sam glances down at her own wearable, fried by the pulse.

"I don't know," he admits, scratching at his nose, "He said something about 'Faraday servers', if that means anything to you?"

Sam shrugs. It doesn't.

"And what about your kit?" she asks.

"Must have been out of range. The city mesh is just about hanging together, though the pulse blew out the core."

Satisfied by his answer, Sam nods wearily. So, it was just a matter of bad luck. Wrong place, wrong time. No longer urban tragedy, but personal slight.

She frowns.

"And what about the IP regime? Don't you think this, this whole thing is kind of dangerous?"

"Well," says Karim, "Apart from the last remnants of the SCA, who is there to enforce the molecular rights? Don't kid yourself, sis, nobody's going to care about our 'national culture' when the city's burning."

She looks down at her feet, as he continues.

"I mean, do you have any idea of the market for these kind of -?"

Silence. She looks up, but he's already gone, darting left, then right, through the narrow alleyways of the dead. On the other side of the clearing, a glint of light reflected off field glasses. Three men in tan uniforms, scanning the landscape for any sign of movement. Acid nausea in the pit of her stomach, Sam leaps back, throwing herself against the rough wall of a crumbling mausoleum. If the blast took out their kit as well, and if she stays put, there's a good chance the Egyptologists won't even see her.

OH, FOR THE LIFE OF A SAILOR!

Paul Graham Raven

I never knew my parents, no sir. But I like to think that if they knew what I was doing now, that they'd be proud of me. I don't blame them for what they did, not any more. I used to, before I joined the Navy.

See, the way I look at it is that they were probably real poor, sir. The orphanage where they left me was right near one of the big *favelas*, and even a dumb Navy boy like me can see that two poor people from the ghettos wouldn't be able to afford to care for someone born the way I was. Sure, there's welfare now, and there was then too - but it still isn't much. It would have been hard for them. Even if they'd been rich folk, I think it would have been hard.

It was even hard for the Sisters at the orphanage … but for all their strictness, sir, they have a lot of care in them, those Sisters. To have raised me to sixteen years of age, an abandoned street boy who couldn't move more than his face, well, it's enough to make me think maybe there's something to their loving Jesus. I don't believe in him, no sir - the things I've seen and been through, it's hard to keep a belief like that. But it sure worked for those Sisters, and they sure worked for me - even with all my anger. And back then, I had a lot of anger.

Well, sir, I had no hope for much more than I already had, and that wasn't much. Even the other kids who were my friends, I was jealous of. How could I not be? They were free, free to move where they chose with nothing more than a thought. Believe me, sir - if thought alone could have moved me then, it would have, because I thought a whole lot about moving. Sometimes I'd be watching from the shade as a smaller kid get jumped in the yard, and I'd envy him the ability to feel the kicks, and to flinch away from them. I got beaten a few times too, but it's no fun beating a kid who doesn't feel it, and who couldn't fight back. Lonely times, sir. Angry times.

So I was pretty rude to the recruiting officer when he came. "How'd you like to join the Navy, son?" he asked. I laughed, and called him a real bad curse-word like the Sisters would punish us for. But he just took it, and asked me again. So I asked him what use the Navy could have for a cripple, and he told me that I shouldn't call myself a cripple, I was just 'physically disadvantaged'. I laughed again, told him that was about right, and asked him what good a physically disadvantaged kid would be on a ship. "We don't want to send you to sea, boy," he said. "How'd you like to go to space?"

Well, I'd never laughed so much in all my life, sir. So hard I cried, and I'd not cried since I was maybe five or six years old. I knew about the Government's space program, working with the Ecuadorians to help build and defend the elevator. I'd seen *los astros*, the big strong heroes in the videos. Every kid dreamed of being picked - even the ones who could move. I thought he was mocking me, sir.

But once he explained what they wanted to do, well, I wasn't laughing any more. I was dead serious, just like him. He'd shown me a door, sir, a way out of a life with no future. A door into space.

It was funny, sir, the way the Sisters tried to talk me out of it. They'd always said they hoped I'd find a way to make my mark on the world, to be happy, but when I told them what I was going to do, they told me Jesus would have thought it was a bad thing. They told the officer that, too, telling him the Navy were bad people, and that Jesus wouldn't think well of them for doing it to me either. But he wasn't bothered, and I was going to be a Navy man, so I decided to act like him and be decisive, too. I listened to their arguments and pleas, and then I signed the papers anyway - the pen gripped so hard in my teeth I nearly broke it - and I let the recruiting officer's junior carry me to the APC outside.

So that's how I came to join the Navy, sir, and I tell you I've never looked back. Because now I'm freer than all those kids I was in the orphanage with, in some ways. Sure, I can't kick a football, or turn cartwheels in the dust at siesta time like they did. I can't stretch out my arm and grab a banana, or shake a hand - and I'll never know what that's like.

But they'll never know what it's like for me, either, sir - what it's like to feel every system and control surface responding as I glide into a matched orbit, to laser debris with a brief thought. I'll never shake hands with a man, but I've docked with my fellow sailors high above the blue ball of the Earth, sir, and pulled into ports most folk will never get to see outside their screens. I can see further than any normal man, fly faster.

I was made for space, sir. The Navy made me for space.

THE LONG WALK AFT
Gareth L Powell

It was Kurt's turn on watch. They were a year out from Earth, forty years from their destination, and it was his turn to be awake.

At first, he enjoyed the solitude. Everyone else was asleep in their pods and he had the ship's echoing corridors to himself. But before long, he grew restless. His duties mainly consisted of checking dials and monitoring the ship's house-keeping systems. As the days began to drag, he started looking forward to the time – six months hence – that he would return to stasis, letting someone else take their turn.

The only thing that relieved the boredom for him was eating. The automatic kitchen could synthesise an impressive range of dishes and delicacies – some familiar, some new and exotic. Each evening he would sit in the mess hall, mouth watering with anticipation, as he waited for his order to appear.

He sampled curries and salads, stews, sandwiches and steaks. Each night he tried something new. Until five weeks into his stint, the kitchen stopped delivering.

Perplexed, he consulted the housekeeping program, only to find that the re-cycling loop had become contaminated – that there were toxins in the biomass the kitchen used to synthesise food.

Without food, he wouldn't last more than a few days. He would have to purge the system and replace the biomass. But where would he get the material to replace it? His bodily wastes could be recycled, but they alone weren't enough to sustain the system. At the very least, he needed a dozen kilograms of organic matter.

He started by collecting together all the leather and cotton he could find, rifling through the clothes stored in the cargo hold. But he was still woefully short of the weight he needed.

He found a couple of wooden bangles; they went into the recycler. There were some books in the captain's cabin, and they went in. But he still didn't have enough.

In desperation, he roamed the ship, eventually ending up in the medical centre. There were some cotton sheets in here that he could use, and he bundled them together, ready to lug back to the recycler. But as he did so, his eye fell on a case of surgical instruments, and a nasty thought entered his head.

He put down the sheets and looked at his left arm. Then he walked over and opened the case, picking out an electric saw. He could cut his arm off just below the shoulder and feed it into the recycler. More would be better, but maybe this sacrifice would suffice. Maybe it would be enough to get the system working again.

He started searching around for anaesthetic, but already knew he couldn't go through with his plan. He was responsible for the safety of the ship. How could he perform his duties with one arm? How could he respond to an emergency if one arose? If he cut his arm off, he'd be jeopardising the well-being of the crew.

He put the saw down. He would have to find another alternative.

But thinking of the crew – all two hundred of them, frozen in their pods in the aft storage section – had already given him another idea.

No, he thought. I can't do that.

But the more he considered it, the more logical and inevitable it became.

So he picked up the saw and revved it. Then he stepped out into the corridor, and with a rumbling stomach and shaking hands, began the long walk aft to where his crewmates slept.

THE GONDOLIER
Gareth D Jones

The black prow of my gondola cut smoothly through the calm waters of the canals. The sleek craft had served me well for many years, carried passengers through the city's waterways under the guiding hands of generations of my forebears.

The sun was setting over the ancient city, turning the water to an inky ribbon lain between elegant sandstone buildings. I breathed deeply of the cool evening breeze.

Was there any place more beautiful than this wondrous city of canals? As the boat eased into its mooring I stopped to gaze with satisfaction up into the darkening skies of Mars.

A KIND OF HOMECOMING
Dan Pawley

There's still time before the shuttle leaves, and so I decide to take a walk outside and say my final goodbyes to Hesperia. Two years I've been here, working out at the other side of the galaxy, and even though I'm going back for good in a few hours, Earth seems further away than ever. I know I'll never pass for a Hesperian, but this place is home to me in a way Earth never was.

I put my bag down on the ground at my feet and lean against one of the wiry dendron trees. When I look up at the purple sky and the weak orange sun I marvel once again at how everything that seemed so strange two years ago can seem so natural today. As if to prove the point, one of the skyrays passes far overhead, its gigantic rubbery wings lazily pushing it through the air. The first time I saw one of those I remember I stood and stared until it was just a tiny dot on the horizon. These days, they're just part of the scenery, and I barely notice them. Not this one though. I watch it navigate the invisible currents of the wind and try to stamp every moment of its passage on my mind, willing myself to remember it.

The cheap colony-built tannoy splutters into life and announces that the shuttle will be departing soon and that all passengers must now head to Emigration. I look back through the glass door and come to a decision. I pick up my bag, pat off the red dust, heft it over my shoulder and walk away from the terminal building, heading out for the horizon.

SATISFACTION
Shaun C Green

He walked between worlds, the traveller, never settling on any one for longer than it took to trade stories. He sought out others who had moved between realities, as he had begun to so long ago. In return he told them of other places he had seen, and shared the tales of others with whom he had made this simple exchange.

Sometimes they would ask him what he sought. He shook his head. "I seek nothing," he told them. "What you see as the act of searching is enough for me."

They would shake their heads and not understand, or nod to feign comprehension. And then they would leave him to his food, or drinks, or his temporary camp in the thoroughfare. They returned home and collected their belongings, vowing to leave this cruel world, and travel on in search of the traveller's tales.

"There's a better world out there," they told their friends and loved ones. "And I'm going to find it."

And off they went, like tortoises with lives on their backs, side-stepping into the place where lines blurred and the other Earths were.

The traveller had, initially, found himself saddened by this. At first he had tried to explain to them that they could not strike out in search of their dreams in this way. Life, he tried to explain, does not work that way. But they refused to believe him.

"This world," they argued, "is so much worse than the one I left. And yet from your own tales I know that a better one exists. You cannot deny it - you have seen it with your own two eyes!"

They would not believe him when he told them they could not get there.

The traveller did not pretend to understand how it worked, this walking-between-worlds, but he knew that he travelled as an almost incidental thing.

He liked to learn new stories, and he liked to tell those he knew. There was little more to it than that.

Yet one thing that he had learned was that every other he had seen, those that struck out in search of a perfect world, a world in which they fit and belonged, would only find themselves betrayed and frustrated. An anarchist with whom he had long ago begun his travels found herself travelling to increasingly dictatorial societies, the ziggurats of hierarchy bearing down on those below growing with each journey. They had parted ways after several such transitions, as she began to wonder if her companion's influence was responsible.

Later, he encountered travelling merchants and late-capitalist entrepreneurs seeking to make their fortunes; these unfortunates found themselves first in places where simple barter economies existed, and money was treated with good-natured derision. Later still they found themselves in societies where commonalities of the people shared what they had freely and willingly.

Those who were private and insular by nature, who sought a place where they might be left alone to live their lives, would only find worlds populated by those who were warm and embracing, who lived in large tribe-like dwellings. Those who sought validation in shared experience, in universal friendship and family, arrived in worlds where people were closed off from one another, societies were eyes were always averted, or where faces were hidden behind featureless masks.

Through them all, through their hopeless dreams and flight toward an imagined perfection, the traveller walked and talked and listened. He never came home, but he made his world as he found it.

ABOUT THE AUTHORS

NEIL BEYNON

Neil is a Welsh writer living in London. Being Welsh means he's around a foot shorter than everyone else, gets far too excited when they beat England at Rugby and thinks football is for people who lack moral fibre. And yes - that is his real hair. He splits his time between a keyboard in Soho, where he works in online marketing, and a keyboard in Abbey Wood, where he does penance for his day job by making up things he hopes other people will enjoy. Occasionally he writes bad poetry. Neil started writing flash fiction when he read GLP's first FFF post; not above jumping on a well-crafted bandwagon, he posted "Shadow", his first flash piece, a few weeks later. It turns out to be more fun than he suspects is strictly legal, and is the most highly read feature of his blog, *The Other Side of the River*. Neil dislikes talking about himself in the third person, as he feels it makes him sound like a bad wrestling promo: If you smeeeelll what he's cooking … you're probably standing too close. Journey to the other side of the river at *http://neilbeynon.wordpress.com*

Neil's stories

SHAUN C GREEN

Shaun Green is a sometime writer living in Brighton on the south coast of England. He's been writing for quite some time. His first published work was a story, with pictures, about Rhubarb and Custard. His mum was very proud. He followed this up with a bestseller about the time a coastguard helicopter came to visit his school. At the time of writing he divides his energies between flash fiction, aborted novels, book reviews and whatever else takes his fancy. This indecisive approach to writing is one reason why he enjoys Friday Flash Fiction so much: there is great scope for experimentation, and feedback is rapidly returned. When not writing Shaun plays guitar in a punk band, works in IT and plays videogames on a variety of platforms. Hot Water Music's 'Jack Of All Trades' is one of his favourite songs. Shaun's blog can be found at *www.nostalgiaforinfinity.com*

Shaun's stories

GARETH D JONES

Gareth D Jones is a science fiction writer from Essex, with stories published both on line and in print and translated into German, Greek, Hebrew and Spanish. Last year he made his first professional sale to *Cosmos* magazine in Australia. He also writes reviews and drinks lots of tea. You can keep an eye on what he's up to at: *http://garethdjones.blogspot.com*

Gareth's stories

DAN PAWLEY

Dan Pawley was born in south-west England in 1972 and, at the time of writing, is still not dead. He makes his living from the tattered corpse of the music industry, and in recent years has lived in the Republic of Ireland, Wales and Japan, all of which conspire to make him sound more interesting than he really is. He always enjoys a nice dystopia and maintains a not-updated-as-often-as-it-should-be blog at *www.bugpowderdust.co.uk*

Dan's stories

JUSTIN PICKARD

For Justin Pickard, the act of finishing his first piece of flash fiction was an act of pure egotism; the final hurdle to be cleared before he could consider himself a 'proper' writer. Since then, semi-regular participation in Friday Flash Fiction has provided literary companionship, much-needed criticism, and an outlet for the more vivid and unsettling details of his dreams.A matter of weeks from completing a degree in Anthropology and International Relations at the University of Sussex, he has spent most of the last three years cultivating a demeanour of vague affability and avoiding the thought of life after graduation. Justin's blog can be found at *http://justinpickard.net*

Justin's stories

GARETH L POWELL

Gareth L Powell graduated from the University of Glamorgan in 1993. He works in software marketing and lives in North Somerset with his wife and daughters. His short stories have been translated into Polish, Portuguese, Spanish, Greek and Hebrew, and adapted for radio in the United States. His first short story collection *The Last Reef* is available from Elastic Press and his first novel *Silversands* will be published by Pendragon Press in 2009. His blog can be found at *http://garethlynpowell.blogspot.com*

Gareth's stories

MARTIN MCGRATH

Martin McGrath is a short, fat, hairy Irishman who sometimes writes short stories. He's had stories published in *Aeon, Jupiter, Scheherazade, Fortean Bureau* and a scattering of other magazines. When he's not doing that, he's editor of *Focus* the BSFA magazine for writers. When he's not doing that he's married to an improbably understanding woman with whom he has a part share in a five year old daughter, who frequently terrifies them both with her grasp of the fundamental nature of the universe. And when he's not doing that, he earns a frankly pitiful living as a journalist/press officer/keyboard for hire. He also blogs, occasionally, at ***www.mmcgrath.co.uk***

Martin's stories

PAUL GRAHAM RAVEN

Paul Graham Raven likes poetry, science fiction stories, music with guitars, and girls with tattoos. His friends play a game that involves them buying him drinks and then steering the conversation round to space colonisation and neural prosthetics. Paul narrowly pays his rent and bills by masquerading as six foot of unkempt part-time museum library assistant. He's also Reviews Editor for *Interzone*, the UK's longest running original science fiction magazine, and recently became Publisher and Editor-in-Chief of veteran science fiction webzine *Futurismic.com*.

He has his own music reviews website, *The Dreaded Press*, and he reviews sf novels for numerous magazines and websites, a full catalogue of which can be found on the "About" page of his blog. The irony is that all of the above are incredibly effective displacement activities for preventing the committing of fiction. Visit Paul at Velcro City Tourist Board – *http://velcro-city.co.uk*

Paul's stories

BSFA

The British Science Fiction Association

AT THE HEART OF FANDOM FOR FIFTY YEARS

The British Science Fiction Association was founded in 1958 to promote the best of science fiction and to bring together fans from all over the United Kingdom.

In 2008 members receive our quarterly magazine *Vector* – a critical joural packed full of features, essays and dozens of book reviews in every issue. Plus there's our twice yearly magazine for writers, *Focus* – which currently features the Masterclass series of articles by Christopher Priest.

There's exclusive online contact at our website, with up-to-the minute film and television reviews, news, interviews, special features and much more. There's our special publications, we've a whole range of unique members' only pamphlets planned for this year. We've got special offers on everything from the latest books to convention membership. And this year we're publishing *Celebrations* - an original anthology of short stories by some of the biggest names in British science fiction.

And don't forget that membership of the BSFA entitles you to free membership of one of our *Orbiter* writers' groups!

If you love science fiction and you're not a member, you're missing out.

For more details, visit our website, and join up now!

WWW.BSFA.CO.UK

All profits from the sale of this book
will go to the NSPCC.
Cruelty to children must stop. FULL STOP.